GOBLIN MARKET

GOBLIN MARKET

by DIANE ZAHLER

HOLIDAY HOUSE · NEW YORK

HOLIDAY HOUSE is registered in the U.S. Patent and Trademark Office.

Printed and bound in June 2022 at Maple Press, York, PA, USA.

www.holidayhouse.com

First Edition

1 3 5 7 9 10 8 6 4 2

Library of Congress Cataloging-in-Publication Data

Names: Zahler, Diane, author.

Title: Goblin market / by Diane Zahler.

Description: First edition. | New York : Holiday House, [2022]
Audience: Ages 8–12. | Audience: Grades 4–6. | Summary: "In this
story inspired by Polish folklore, two sisters face a goblin prince in
the dark forest"–Provided by publisher.

Identifiers: LCCN 2021053819 | ISBN 9780823450817 (hardcover)
ISBN 9780823452927 (ebook)

Subjects: CYAC: Sisters–Fiction. | Goblins–Fiction. | Love–Fiction.
Magic–Fiction. | LCGFT: Novels.

Classification: LCC PZ7.Z246 Go 2022 | DDC [Fic]–dc23

LC record available at https://lccn.loc.gov/2021053819

ISBN: 978-0-8234-5081-7 (hardcover)

In loving memory of Pooh

For Ben
Bądź sobą!

For there is no friend like a sister

In calm or stormy weather;

To cheer one on the tedious way,

To fetch one if one goes astray,

To lift one if one totters down,

To strengthen whilst one stands.

–Christina Rossetti

CHAPTER 1

Market day was Lizzie's favorite day of the week.

Not because she loved *going* to the market–the few times she'd been there, she'd hated it. There were so many people she didn't know, from villages and farms clear on the other side of Elza. So much noise, such constant comings and goings, so many smells and colors! It was overwhelming, terrifying. Each time she'd ended up hiding in a doorway at the edge of the square, trembling, until Mother and Minka came to find her.

Now Minka went to market on her own.

Mother was delighted that Minka was old enough to go alone: she could stay home and attend to the chores. And Lizzie was delighted that she could steal into the Wood for an hour or two when she was done helping Father in the fields.

In the Wood, Lizzie always went to the same place, a little stand of birch trees beside a trickling stream. If it was warm and the sun shone down onto the circle of grass inside the grove, she would lie and look up at the sky. She could feel the breath of the Wood as the wind rustled the birch leaves. She could hear the Wood's chuckle in the water running over rocks. Sometimes she felt as if the Wood's heart thrummed inside her body. Her own pulse matched the Wood's, beat for beat.

If it was cold, she would wrap up in her shawl and walk to stay warm, just listening–to bird songs, to the creak of branches rubbing together, to the rustle of rabbits and squirrels in the underbrush.

For Lizzie, each sound was a color. When she was younger, seven or eight, she'd sat at the kitchen table and tried to paint what she heard, but Minka laughed and pointed at her painted trees, saying, "Leaves aren't gray, silly! And those don't even look like trees. They look like sticks with clouds on top." Minka loved to paint. She did it whenever she had a few minutes free of chores, and sometimes instead of chores. She mostly used watercolors, but if she had a few extra coppers, she would go into Elza and buy a tube of oil paint–cerulean blue, or chartreuse, or violet–and paint the whitewashed walls of the cottage with flowers and intricate designs, inside and out. Her lips were always tinted blue or green because she chewed on her brushes when she thought about what to paint.

"We don't have any silver paint," Lizzie said. "I had to use gray."

"Leaves aren't silver, either," Minka pointed out. "They're green. Or red and orange in the autumn." She took the paintbrush, dipped it, and in a few moments there was a tree on the paper, brown and green and almost as real as life.

"But the sound the leaves make is silver," Lizzie protested. "In springtime, anyway."

Minka rolled her eyes. "What does that even mean?" she asked. "*The sound the leaves make is silver*?"

"It's the color they make when they rustle together," Lizzie said. "When the breeze blows. You know, the wavery lines of silver?"

Minka's face was blank.

"You don't see that?" Lizzie was confused. The idea that other people didn't see what she saw was new to her.

"You *do* see that? Actually see it?"

Lizzie nodded.

Minka stared at her sister. "Describe it to me, exactly."

Minka put down a new sheet of paper and picked up her paints again, blending and daubing as Lizzie spoke. And when she was done, the tree was on paper, just as Lizzie saw it. She clapped her hands with joy, and Minka laughed and dabbed her on the nose with the silvery color she had somehow managed to create from the paints she had. Ever since, Lizzie had explained the colors she saw to Minka, and Minka painted what Lizzie described. Those paintings hung beside Minka's wall art, in wooden frames that Father carved during the long winter nights—a bear in a cloud of deep burgundy, the color of its rumbling growl; the teakettle whistling bright copper steam; yellow-green rain falling on their cottage.

"Such strange colors!" Mother would say, shaking her head. But Father liked them.

It was July and warm in the Wood today, almost hot. The birch trees shaded Lizzie, and she lay for a few minutes on the Wood's chest and listened to its heartbeat. A hawk flew overhead, invisible beyond the thick treetops, its high-pitched call oddly shrill in such a powerful bird. She had to close her eyes, the red vortex of its screech was so intense. As it faded, she rested quietly, watching the silver smoke sound of the rustling leaves rise amid the branches.

When the sun began to sink and the air cooled a little, Lizzie stood up, brushed the grass from her skirt, and started back home. As always, she met Minka as she returned from market. When her sister saw Lizzie, she shook her head.

"How do you always know I'm coming?" she asked. "Do you listen for me?"

Lizzie shrugged. "I just know," she said, pulling a piece of carrot from her pocket and offering it to Kosmy, the donkey. He took it with his enormous front teeth and chewed it loudly, smacking his donkey lips. The girls led him to the small thatched-roof stable beside the kitchen garden and unhitched him. He tried to stick his nose in Minka's pocket, looking for more food. He was always hungry.

"I sold all the bread," Minka reported, pushing the donkey away. "And the peppers and the beans. Mistress Agata had tomatoes."

"That's early," Lizzie said. "Ours won't be ripe for weeks yet." She looked closely at Minka. Something seemed a little different. Her face had a light flush. Her words, too, were a little brighter than usual—the wild strawberry color from Minka's paint palette, rather than her usual rose pink. "Do you feel all right?"

"I'm fine," Minka said. "Better than fine, actually."

"Better than fine? What does that mean?"

Minka smiled. Her eyes sparkled in a way that made Lizzie nervous. "It means we sold all the bread, of course!"

"And what else?" Minka almost always sold all the bread. Their bread was very good, light and crusty with what Mistress Agata, who rarely gave a compliment, called a "delicate crumb."

"Minka!" Mother opened the cottage door and came out to inspect the cart, wiping her hands on the towel tucked into her apron. "I see you've done quite well today—except for the squashes." There was a small pile of yellow and green summer squashes still in the cart.

"Everyone has squashes," Minka said. "Too many squashes. You know how it is this time of year."

Lizzie sighed. It would be squash fritters, squash pudding, pierogies stuffed with squash until autumn. Every year they ate squash until they were sick of it.

Mother gathered the zucchinis in her apron and

took them inside, calling, "Come and help me grate them, Lizzie!"

"Coming," Lizzie said, and then to Minka again, "And what else?"

"Oh, nothing much," Minka replied, brushing the dust of the lane off her flounced white underskirt. "There were some new people there today, from the north."

"New people?" Lizzie didn't much care for the old people. It was just like Minka to be pleased about new ones.

"They sold fruit. Some of it was gorgeous. The plums—oh, you'd have loved them."

Lizzie did love plums. "Did you buy any?"

Minka shook her head. "Mother said not to buy anything today. But one of them gave me a purple plum, just to try. So I'd buy next time. I'm sorry I didn't save it for you. I just couldn't. It smelled so wonderful—I had to eat it." She closed her eyes and smiled dreamily, remembering.

Lizzie frowned. It wasn't like Minka to get worked up over fruit. She liked cookies and press cake; pączki filled with cream; tarts and candies. The more sugar the better. Fruit wasn't sweet enough for her.

"Who gave you the plum?" she asked. Minka's eyes opened and she blushed a deeper rose.

"Oh, I don't know," she said, offhanded. Her words shimmered. "Just a boy."

"A *boy*?"

Minka took a deep breath. "Yes, a boy!" she said, all in a rush. "The handsomest boy you've ever seen. Beautiful, almost. And nice. And funny!"

Lizzie was silent, but Minka couldn't stop. Her words tumbled out like water released from a dam.

"He gave me the plum because he said he didn't have any peaches, but my skin was like a peach, and a plum was the next-best thing, and when I ate it, *oh,* it was delicious! I never tasted anything like it. And the juice ran all down my chin—it was so embarrassing! But he had a fine linen handkerchief and he wiped it away. And then when I was done he took the pit and dug a little hole in the ground and put it in, and he said a plum tree would grow there, and we would always know exactly where we had first met."

Lizzie blinked. Minka had never talked about a boy this way before.

Of course, all the boys they knew—Jakob and Stefan and Jacek and Eryk—were like brothers: they'd grown up with them, seen their runny noses and

8

their scab-picking, seen Jakob wetting his pants when he was five. Minka would never sound dreamy about any of them.

"Plums are purple," Lizzie said. "So he was saying you have purple skin."

"Oh, Lizzie, stop! It was the *next-best thing.* He said I was like a peach!"

This was almost as strange to Lizzie. A peach was orange, and Minka's skin was a translucent ivory pink. And peaches were fuzzy. Minka's face was as smooth as glass.

"And you've stained your blouse," Lizzie noted. Minka looked down at her blouse and the dark stain across the front.

"It was the plum juice," she said. "But I know you can get it out. You always do."

Laundry was Lizzie's chore. She'd never admit it, but she loved doing it. The rhythm of scrubbing, the precision of folding, the challenge of getting every shirt and skirt and kerchief perfectly clean. She was extremely good at it, and she knew it. But she wouldn't let Minka's compliment distract her.

"What is plum boy's name?" she pressed.

Minka smiled. "Emil," she said. "His name is Emil. Isn't that a lovely name?"

"Elzbieta!" Mother called through the open window to Lizzie. "Come in right now!" When Mother used Lizzie's whole name, she meant business.

"Not a word to Mother and Father about Emil," Minka said urgently. "Do you promise?"

Lizzie gave her a skeptical look. But it was Minka asking. "All right, I promise," she said. Then she added, "You'd better put the cart away and feed Kosmy." *Emil.* It was an ordinary name, a stupid name. It sounded greenish brown to her, even though when Minka said it, it had a cherry-pink hue.

Emil. Minka had met a boy.

They didn't mention the plum or Emil to Mother or Father, of course. Minka drifted through supper, picking at her stew and rye dumplings and smiling at nothing in a way that Lizzie found annoying. After the meal, Mother took out the mending, and to escape the stuffy air indoors and the tedium of the mending basket, Lizzie and Minka offered to weed the garden.

They walked through the neat rows of vegetables hanging heavy on their vines, Minka humming as Lizzie slapped at gnats that buzzed their way into her hair and onto her eyelashes. Occasionally one of the girls bent to pull up a weed. Finally Lizzie ventured, "Will you see him again next week? Emil?"

"Oh yes!" Minka said, snapping off a peapod and scraping the sweet peas into her mouth. "He'll be there." She handed a second peapod to Lizzie, but Lizzie batted it away. "He had such fruits, Lizzie! You can't imagine. There were things I'd never seen before. And apples, in July. Ripe ones! Really, you should come and see for yourself."

Lizzie shook her head, setting a swarm of gnats aflight. "I don't think so."

Minka looked at her sister, her gaze clear for the first time all evening. "Because you're afraid? Lizzie, you must try to get over your worries. You're scared of everything! What will you do later on, when I go to work or marry? You'll be the one going to market then. Isn't it best to get used to it now?"

Lizzie was taken aback. Her *worries,* as Mother called them, were something she and Minka almost never spoke about. Mother and Father often scolded her for refusing to go to town, or to the occasional parties in the Town Hall, but Minka always took her side. "Lizzie will go when she's ready," she'd say, rubbing her sister's arm. "There's no rush." Mother would purse her lips, Father would shake his head, but they'd leave off. They remembered the one dance they'd insisted she go to, two years before. It had been unspeakably awful.

"Are you going to marry Emil, then?" Lizzie asked. She tried to make the question sound mocking, but her voice was a little unsteady.

Minka didn't seem to notice. "Silly," she said fondly. "We've only just met. And I'm far too young to marry." But her small, satisfied smile said something else entirely.

"And it's not fair to say that I'm afraid of everything," Lizzie added. "I'm not afraid of snakes, and you are."

"That's true," Minka said with a little shiver. "Though I'm not so afraid of them as Jakob is!" It was a snake that had scared Jakob—their nearest neighbor—so much that he'd wet himself, years and years ago when they were all small. Everyone still teased him about it, but he was good-natured. He even laughed when someone brought it up.

"And I'm not afraid of the dark," Lizzie pointed out. "Or...or..." It should be easier to think of things she didn't fear, she knew. But there were a lot of scary things in the world.

"What about people?" Minka asked gently. "Thunderstorms? Hugs?"

Lizzie looked down at the ground and took a deep breath. "I'll think about going to market," she said. "Not next week, though. Maybe the week after." She bent and tore out a weed savagely.

"That's a good start. It won't be so very bad. And don't worry. I'll be right there with you." Minka said this all the time, but often it was very bad indeed. She patted Lizzie's shoulder, but Lizzie shrugged her off, refusing to look up. "Don't be like that! You know it will always be Lizzie and Minka, me and you."

Lizzie was silent.

"Come on, Lizzie. Say it, please! *Lizzie and Minka, me and you.*"

"*Even when we're ancient crones,*" Lizzie said reluctantly, standing and reciting the next line of the song they'd composed together, years before.

"*Rocking in our ancient chairs—*"

"*Grumbling ancient pea-green groans—*"

"*Combing out our ancient hairs—*"

"*Lizzie and Minka, just we two!*" they ended together. Minka clapped her hands in satisfaction, and Lizzie finally smiled. She tossed aside her handful of weeds and headed back to the cottage with her sister.

CHAPTER 2

Lizzie watched Minka closely all that week. She worried as she did the laundry on Monday, scrubbing and scrubbing to get the plum juice stain out of Minka's ruffled white blouse. She fretted as she helped Father in the fields, readying the wheat for harvest.

Even the piercing calls of the red-winged blackbirds down by the river couldn't calm her. Usually she loved the scarlet of their cries, so like the flash of color on their black wings. Theirs was one of the very few sounds that was the same color as its source, and that pleased her. But not that week.

She noted when Minka drifted off from her chores or conversations into a reverie. She saw when Minka burned the bread or tripped over Marek the cat or set her dishcloth afire over the stove. She peered over her sister's shoulder as Minka tried to paint Emil, though every attempt ended in a streak of black across the paper before Minka, frustrated, crumpled it and threw it on the fire.

But as the days passed, Minka seemed to become more anxious and less dreamy. By the time Friday market day came, she was a twitchy bundle of nerves, snapping at Lizzie, brushing Marek off her lap as he sat comfortably grooming himself, even yanking at Kosmy's bridle as she hitched him up.

"You seem a little...tense," Lizzie observed, piling neatly wrapped loaves of bread into the cart.

"Not at all," Minka retorted. "I'm just hot. It's very warm today." Kosmy turned his head and gave her a skeptical look.

Minka's nervousness made Lizzie nervous, too, and she wondered if she should offer to go with her sister after all. But the thought was terrifying. Every time she considered it, her stomach sank and a cold sweat broke out on her forehead. She couldn't begin to imagine how she would keep her promise to Minka to accompany her next week. She wasn't ready. She would never be ready.

"Will you be all right?" Lizzie asked. Her worry must have shown in her voice, even to Minka, who couldn't see its colors.

"I'll be fine," Minka said, rubbing Lizzie's arm. That was her way of hugging her sister. "Really I will. I'll see you in a few hours."

"I'll be waiting," Lizzie said, and Minka flashed her a tight smile.

"I know you will!"

Lizzie always waved as Minka trudged down the lane toward Elza, and Minka always turned at the curve in the road and waved back. But today the cart just kept on, and Minka didn't turn. The break from their routine made Lizzie uneasy. She wrapped her arms around herself and waited for a moment, hoping her sister would realize she hadn't waved and come back, but the lane was empty except for the little cloud of dust that Kosmy had kicked up.

Lizzie spent the morning in the fields with Father, toiling side by side in the silence they favored. They worked together well, whether they were ploughing with Kosmy, planting seeds up and down the rows, hoeing the weeds away, pulling up potatoes and beets, or scything the golden wheat when it was harvest time. When they grew too hot they would rest in the shade of a massive oak tree, drinking spring-water from the jug Mother gave them and eating her special poppy seed cookies. Sometimes Father would sing an old folk song from his childhood, his voice rising carmine red and dissipating among the leaves of the oak as Lizzie lay comfortably on the mossy ground.

Later, in the Wood after sweaty hours in the fields, Lizzie couldn't settle. She sat for a moment in her little glade, but the sound of her own lilac heartbeat in her ears drowned out any sound the Wood might have made. She skipped a rock into the stream, then wandered about for a while, picking flowers and dropping them aimlessly. Minka was right; it was very hot. She headed back to the stream to dip her feet in the cool water, but a crashing through the bushes behind her made her spin around in alarm.

"Lizzie!" It was Jakob. Tagging along behind him, as always, was his little brother, Stefan, a half-sized copy of Jakob: the same dark hair and eyes and sun-browned skin, the same impish gap-toothed smile.

"Oh," Lizzie said, her hand on her heart. "It's just you."

"Just me," Jakob said. He grinned, and the space between his front teeth comforted her.

"Just us!" Stefan echoed.

"*Just me* hasn't seen just you in a long time," Jakob said.

Lizzie saw them every day in the one-room schoolhouse during the late fall and winter, but it wasn't often that they met outside school. Their father was known for his strictness, and the boys had to finish their work to his satisfaction before they could take any time for themselves.

"What have you and your beautiful sister been doing?" Jakob asked.

"Beautiful?" Lizzie said doubtfully. "Do you think Minka is beautiful?"

Jakob sat on the mossy bank of the stream and motioned to Lizzie to sit next to him. He pulled off his boots and sank his feet into the water. Stefan tossed his own boots aside and jumped in with both feet, splashing Jakob and Lizzie.

"Oh, that feels good," Jakob said. He took a kerchief from his shirt pocket, dipped it in the water, and wiped his face, leaving a streak of cleaner skin where the cloth passed. "It's hot and dusty in the fields today, I can tell you! Sorry if my feet stink, by the way."

"They're a little smelly," Lizzie said, pulling off her own boots, and Jakob laughed.

"I can always count on you to tell me the truth!" he said.

Lizzie kicked her feet in the water. It made a lovely lavender splash-sound, and droplets arced in the sunlight. "So...Minka is beautiful?" she asked again, watching Stefan try to catch a frog along the far bank. Every time he jumped, hands outstretched, the frog jumped just far enough to escape him.

"Well, sure," Jakob said, surprised. "That yellow hair, those big eyes—everybody thinks so. Don't you?"

Lizzie pondered this. "I guess she is," she said. "I never really thought about it. I thought beautiful people were supposed to be stuck-up."

"Some of them are," Jakob agreed. "Like Zofia. I asked her to dance at the last harvest ball, and she looked at me like...well, like my feet stank. And my boots were on!"

Lizzie giggled. Jakob was one of the few people who could make her laugh. He didn't give her that look other people did when she said something unexpected, or backed away from a touch, or refused to speak in school. It wasn't so much that he understood her; he just didn't mind. However a person was, that was fine with Jakob.

"Minka isn't like that."

"No," Jakob said. "She's nice to everyone. Even Stefan." Stefan was a terrible pest, forever trailing after the older children, but Minka always found a way to let him join in their games.

"Oh," Lizzie said, pulling her feet from the water, "Minka will be coming back any minute from the market. I have to meet her." She tugged her boots back on.

"And we should get back to work," Jakob said. "Pa will be furious that we've been gone so long. But Stefan was starting to get wobbly in the heat, so I wanted him to sit in the shade for a bit. And see how he sits!" He pointed at his little brother as Stefan slipped off a mossy rock into waist-deep water, and they both laughed.

"Come and say hello to Minka," Lizzie invited. "I know she'd be glad to see you."

Jakob busied himself putting on his boots. "Oh, I don't think so."

"You shouldn't go back into the fields yet," Lizzie said. "Your face is all red. You'll get sunstroke."

Jakob wet his handkerchief again and scrubbed

his face. "There," he said. "Is that better?" But he was still red, and Lizzie wondered if it was just the sun.

"Come on," she insisted, and reluctantly Jakob nodded.

"Get your boots, Stef!" he called, and Stefan splashed over to them. He refused to put on his heavy boots, though, so barefoot he followed them to the lane before Lizzie's house.

In a moment they heard Kosmy's hoofbeats and the rattle of Minka's cart as they rounded the curve. Minka seemed almost to be dancing as she urged the overheated donkey on. "Move, move, you stubborn fellow!" she cried. Her voice was high-pitched, her words nearly fuchsia.

"Oh, *Lizzie*!" she exclaimed as Kosmy ambled determinedly at his own deliberate pace. "Wait till you hear!" Then she noticed Jakob and Stefan. "Jakob! Where have you been all summer? I've hardly seen you!"

Jakob looked down and kicked up a little cloud of dust. "I've been in the fields," he mumbled. "Working. You know."

Minka laughed, a little shrilly. "Of course you have! How silly of me!"

Lizzie looked in the cart. There were piles of

vegetables, and even some bread. "Minka, you didn't sell much."

"I didn't, did I?" Minka agreed. "I hope Mother isn't upset. But I was...busy."

"Busy? With Emil?"

Jakob looked up. "Emil? Who's that?"

"He's a *boy*," Lizzie said, trying to make *boy* sound ominous. "From north of town. He sells fruit."

"He does indeed," Minka said. "Lizzie, he had even more this time. I learned the names of some of the strange ones. He had dewberries, and bullaces, and pomegranates—oh, the pomegranates! They have little syrupy crunchy seeds—it's like biting into sweetness itself."

"I've heard of pomegranates," Jakob said. "But they don't grow around here. And what on earth is a bullace?"

"Bullace, bullace, bollocks," Stefan chanted. "Minka, look how dirty my feet are!" He kicked up a bare foot, covered with dust that had clung to the stream-wetness.

But Minka ignored him. "A bullace is like a plum," she said. Her face changed, remembering.

"Did you bring some home?" Lizzie asked.

"No, I ate them there. With Emil."

Lizzie frowned. She would have liked to try the pomegranate. "Did you buy them?"

"Well..." Minka's voice trailed off. "Not exactly."

"What do you mean?"

Minka flushed. "He wouldn't take any money. He only wanted—well, he wanted a lock of my hair."

Lizzie's mouth made a little O. "You didn't!"

"It was just a strand or two," Minka said defensively. Even Jakob seemed shocked, and Stefan looked up from his dirty feet.

"You cut off your hair to give to a boy?" he asked, interested. "Why?"

Minka frowned. "Never mind. It's none of your business. Come on, Lizzie, let's unload the cart."

Mother came outside then, and she greeted the boys with pleasure. When she saw what was left in the cart, though, she was less than pleased. "I hope you'll do better next week" was all she said. Minka withered under her stern gaze.

Mother turned to Jakob and Stefan with a smile. "Boys, would you like to take supper with us?"

Stefan's eyes lit up, but Jakob quickly shook his head. "Oh, I don't think—"

A shout in the distance interrupted him. "Jakob! Stefan! Get over here *now*!"

Stefan gave a little squeak, and Lizzie looked down the lane. Jakob and Stefan's pa stood in the middle of the broad path, thick and stolid, his face red in the afternoon sunlight, his hands on his hips. He frightened Lizzie. His voice was always a harsh purple, the color that on Minka's palette was labeled PURPUREUS. It was a nasty color, and he was a nasty man.

"Uh-oh," Jakob breathed. "Thank you, ma'am, but we'd better be going." He grabbed Stefan by the hand and yanked him forward. Lizzie watched as they ran home, wincing as their pa smacked Jakob on the side of the head as he passed.

"Master Nowak is so mean!" Minka breathed when they'd disappeared from sight around the bend.

"He's a hard, sad man," Mother said, shaking her head. "I feel for those boys."

Supper was a quiet meal, and Lizzie noticed Minka's flushed cheeks giving way to a strange pallor. As soon as they were finished with the dishes, Minka climbed the ladder to the loft where she and Lizzie slept. Lizzie did the rest of her chores and Minka's without protest. When she climbed up herself, Minka had turned in the bed to face the wall. She breathed evenly, but Lizzie could tell she wasn't asleep.

"Minka," she whispered. "Minka, I know you're awake. Talk to me." But Minka refused to answer, and Lizzie lay and wondered until she drifted off into an uneasy sleep.

❦

The morning dawned sunless and ominous. An approaching thunderstorm threatened to break the heat wave, and it pushed before it a wind that hissed yellow-taupe around the house, making the shutters flap and tossing the clean clothes off the line into the dust.

"Girls!" Mother called from the doorway. "Help me get the clothes in before the storm!"

Minka moaned and turned over. The light from the loft window made her skin even more sallow than the night before. Lizzie touched her sister's forehead with her hand. It was warm—far too warm.

"I'll go," she said. "I'll tell Mother you're sick."

"Thank you," Minka whispered.

Lizzie pulled on her skirt and blouse and scrambled down the ladder. She stopped at the basin to splash her face with water and tie back her hair, then followed her mother outside into the wind. Immediately her skin was gritty with dust from the road, and her eyes watered from it.

"Where is your sister?" Mother demanded as they pulled clothes from the line and dumped them haphazardly into the wicker basket.

"She's sick. I think she has a fever."

Mother sighed. "Oh dear. A summer fever is never good. I'll take a look at her when we go in."

They finished just as the first crack of thunder sounded, and Lizzie jumped. How she hated thunderstorms! The sounds were so loud and so unpredictable. She couldn't even tell for sure what colors they would be. It depended on the distance, the strength of the storm, the volume of the thunderclaps. A thunderstorm was never a single color; it was a vortex of colors, sometimes spinning so quickly that Lizzie would become dizzy and nauseated and have to sit down. Minka had painted a storm for her once as she described it, its whirling colors ranging from indigo on the outside to a sickly greenish gold in the center, but when the painting was finished, Lizzie had begged their father not to hang it up. She couldn't bear to look at it.

Safely inside, Lizzie and Mother folded the clothes. Minka climbed down the ladder to help them, but Mother waved her off. "Sit and rest, child," she said.

"We have enough hands for this. You shouldn't fool with a summer fever."

The storm changed to a steady rain that kept up all day. A cool breeze blew damply through the open windows, and Minka began to look a little better. She ate a bit and drank tea, and some color came back to her cheeks. Mother felt her forehead.

"I believe the fever is down," she said. "Minka, you can join us for the mending this afternoon. I don't believe we'll get outside until tomorrow."

"Poor Father," Lizzie said. He had to tend the fields, rain or no rain. She didn't help him when there was a chance of thunder.

"He's better off when it's cool and rainy than when it's as hot as it's been," Mother said sensibly. "He can always change wet clothes and wash off mud." She pulled a sock with a hole in the heel from the mending basket and handed it to Lizzie, who was terrible at darning socks. Mother always told her she'd improve with practice, but it didn't seem likely. Her socks usually ended up with a knobby bulge where she'd stitched—one that rubbed in boots and caused nasty blisters. Minka wouldn't even let Lizzie touch her socks anymore.

After supper, Minka's fever rose again, and by the next morning she was red and damp with perspiration, though the air outside and in was much fresher. Mother brought her down to the sofa in the main room and bathed her brow in cool water throughout the day, while Lizzie tended to as many of their chores as she could manage—sweeping, mixing the bread dough and setting it to rise, washing the dishes. When Mother began to prepare supper, Lizzie took over the brow-bathing. Minka lay with her eyes closed. Her breathing seemed heavy and labored.

"Minka," Lizzie said, her voice low. "Are you sick because of the fruit you ate?" She looked at Mother to be sure she hadn't heard, but she was busy cutting up potatoes.

"I don't think so," Minka answered. Her words came out slowly. "None of it was rotted. It all tasted delicious. And my stomach doesn't hurt. I just feel... oh, I don't know. Tired, I guess, and weak."

"Then was someone at the market sick? Did you get this from Emil?"

"No!" Minka said emphatically. "He was at the very peak of health. Surely I'd have known if he was ill, don't you think?"

"I suppose so." But Lizzie wasn't certain. A boy

who asked a girl to cut off her hair as payment for food…that was, she thought, not a nice boy. Not a boy who would be careful around a girl when he was sick.

Lizzie ran her fingers through her sister's luxurious long hair, trying to figure out where the lost lock had come from. As she did, she noticed something odd, and she bent closer.

"Minka," she whispered. "Some of your hair…it looks gray."

Minka's eyes fluttered open. "What?"

"Here, at your temples. Your hair is gray."

"That's absurd." Minka pushed herself upright on the sofa. "Bring me my brush and mirror. Let me see."

Lizzie scurried up the ladder and back. She gave the mirror to Minka, perched beside her, and began pulling the brush through her sister's hair. Minka loved to have her hair brushed, and Lizzie loved to brush the golden weight of it. She did it nearly every night. As Lizzie brushed, Minka moved the mirror this way and that, holding out strands of hair to see them more clearly.

"I think it's the light," she said. "I don't think it's gray at all." But she sounded uncertain.

Then Lizzie cried out, her voice filled with horror.

Minka froze, and Mother turned from the stove to look at her. "What is it, child?" she asked, wiping her hands on her apron.

But Lizzie was speechless.

She simply held up the hairbrush, clumps of yellow hair dangling from it.

Minka screamed, clapping her hands to her head. But it was too late. Much of her hair had separated from her scalp, and it lay in a mound on Lizzie's lap, like a fairy-tale pile of straw that had been spun into gold.

CHAPTER 3

Lizzie leapt to her feet, and the hair and brush went flying.

Summoned by the scream, Father burst in from the garden. His eyes widened as he stared at Minka, her once-glorious golden locks now sparse and streaked with gray. Mother came running, too, as Minka collapsed—crumpled and motionless—on the sofa, her cheeks ashen. Mother held her daughter, but Minka was too distraught to speak.

"We must ask Dr. Śmigly to come in the morning," Mother said faintly.

Lizzie gathered the hair that had fallen from her lap to the floor. She could only remember Dr. Śmigly coming to the cottage once before, when Father had slipped on the rain-slick roof as he replaced cracked shingles and fallen to the ground, breaking his leg. To be sure, she was a fine doctor—Father didn't even limp after the bone healed—but she was only called for true emergencies.

Lizzie was beginning to feel frightened. She had never heard of a sickness that made a person's hair fall out. They'd all had fevers before, but Minka's... Minka's was different.

Minka spent the night on the sofa; Mother didn't want her to risk a dizzy spell going up or down the ladder to the loft. Lizzie couldn't sleep well without her sister's soft breathing as a lullaby. She dozed uneasily all night.

In the morning, Lizzie climbed down the ladder as soon as she heard Mother stirring.

"How is she?" she whispered, looking at Minka. Her sister slept motionless on the sofa, wrapped in a blanket. Despite the heat of the fire and the morning air, there was no sweat beaded on her forehead.

"She shivered half the night through," Mother said in a low voice. "I couldn't keep her warm. But she's sleeping now. Go on to the doctor. Tell her what's happened."

Lizzie grabbed a slice of bread and headed out the door and down the lane to Dr. Śmigly's house. She had never been there before, but she knew it was the trim little cottage with the window boxes spilling vivid pansies, just beyond the schoolhouse.

She paused before knocking. Knocking on people's doors wasn't something she did. Visiting people she didn't know well wasn't something she did. But the image of Minka's pale face, her stringy grayish hair, made Lizzie lift the door knocker and let it go. It hit the door loudly, a vivid turquoise swath of sound in the quiet morning.

The doctor must have been an early riser. She answered the door almost immediately, wearing a long robe, her hair tied up in a flowered kerchief. As soon as she saw Lizzie's face, she ushered her inside.

"Sit, child. I'll be ready in a minute. Is it your father?" She moved quickly into a back room.

"No, my sister. Minka," Lizzie called back. "She has a fever. Her hair fell out."

There was a silence. Then Dr. Śmigly said, "There's tea brewing in the pot if you want some."

"No, thank you," Lizzie replied. She gazed around at the rich-looking carpets, the ornately carved wooden bookcases crammed with volumes. An inlaid table held a teapot and more piles of books. Long, dusty green drapes covered the windows and puddled on the floor. It was a strange room, completely different from the painted rooms in her own cottage, where the furniture was simple and well used and the curtains were hand-tatted lace. But something about it appealed to her. It looked like the room of someone who spent a lot of time thinking.

The doctor came out, dressed and carrying a bag. She wore a pair of round glasses perched on the end of her nose.

"All right, child—Elzbieta, is it?"

"Yes. Lizzie," Lizzie said.

The doctor led Lizzie to the door. She stopped so suddenly that Lizzie nearly crashed into her.

"My glasses," she said. "Where did I leave them?" She spun around, surveying the room, and Lizzie watched her curiously.

"Um...they're on your face," she said.

Dr. Śmigly put her hand up to feel them. "So they are," she said. "If they'd been a snake, they would have bitten me! One of these days I'll have to get a chain for them: they're either lost or I've forgotten I'm wearing them, always. If they were around my neck..."

Lizzie nodded politely. She had a feeling the doctor might forget the glasses were on a chain if she had one.

As they hurried down the road, Lizzie nearly had to run to keep up with Dr. Śmigly. Her legs were long, and she strode without looking left or right. When they passed Jakob's father's fields, they saw the brothers and their father out hoeing. All three looked up with curiosity, but Lizzie only gave a brief wave and hastened on. They reached the cottage quickly, and Lizzie opened the door for the doctor. Mother stood just inside, looking panicked.

"She's delirious," Mother said, her voice quavering. "She keeps talking about outlandish people, and food. She cries out for fruit. Fruit! Oh, Doctor, what's wrong with her?"

The doctor put a soothing hand on Mother's arm. "Calm yourself," she said. "A delirious person will feel the strain in your words and worsen. Speak to her as you would to a frightened child. She *is* frightened, I've no doubt, in whatever strange place her mind is wandering." She hurried over to the sofa, set down her bag, and knelt beside Minka. Lizzie was shocked to see Father standing in a corner of the room, his face worried. Father was never indoors at this time on a summer day.

"Ah, good, you've kept her nice and warm," the doctor said. "Now, Minka, how are you feeling this fine day? It's sunny. We must get you better so you can enjoy it." She kept up a patter of soothing words that washed through the room in a pale melon color. Lizzie felt her own quick pulse slowing. Minka thrashed and moaned at first, but then she, too, quieted.

"That's better, that's good," the doctor murmured. She listened to Minka's heart, felt around her neck and jaw, raised and lowered her arms and legs. Minka stayed as limp as a rag doll. When the doctor was finished, she smoothed Minka's hair–what was left of it–then rose and came into the kitchen, where Mother sat at the round wooden table. Father came out from his corner and sat, too, Lizzie hovering beside him.

The doctor's face was grave. "I do not know what her ailment is," she said. "But I think I've seen it before."

"You have? Where?" Father demanded. "Did you cure it then?"

Dr. Śmigly sighed. "Do you remember a girl called Janina? From a village to the north?"

Mother thought for a moment. Then her hand flew to cover her mouth, and Lizzie saw Father's face darken.

"She died," he said shortly.

"Yes," Dr. Śmigly said. "I was new to the job of doctoring then, and they called me in after old Dr. Belza from her own village had failed to help her. Like Minka, she'd aged strangely and faded, growing weaker by the day. When I saw her, she had only hours left to live. I couldn't save her."

Mother moaned, the sound a puff of dull blue-green smoke rising into the air.

"There must be something you can do!" Father exclaimed. "You never learned what was wrong with Janina? What sickness she had?"

Dr. Śmigly shook her head. "I never found out. Her parents said she kept talking about fruit, though, just like Minka. I am trying to recall. Was it grapes…? Eventually, I decided it must have been a fungus that made her ill—something brought in on fruit from far away. But there was no proof."

Lizzie shivered. Grapes. Or maybe it was plums. And Janina had *died*.

"Minka ate some fruit," she said. The adults turned to look at her. "At the market."

"Ah," Dr. Śmigly said, nodding. "A connection. That's good. I will assume, then, that this is indeed the result of a fungus of some sort. There must be a spoiled batch of fruit being sold."

"Can you treat that?" Mother breathed. Father put a hand on her shoulder. His fingers, crusted with dirt from the fields that never washed off completely, trembled on the thin cotton of her blouse.

"We can try," Dr. Śmigly said firmly. "Do you have cabbage seeds?"

Mother blinked and turned to Lizzie. "Do we?"

"In the cellar," Lizzie said. "I'll go. How much do you need?"

"A small spoon's worth," the doctor instructed.

Lizzie hurried to the door that led down into the dark root cellar, throwing it open and making her way down the rickety stairs. A wooden frame held boxes of seeds for the late-summer planting. She pulled out the cabbage seed box and poured a small heap of seeds into her palm, then climbed back up the stairs.

"A little wine, boiled," the doctor said. Mother started to rise, but Father quickly found the wine jug under the sink and poured a cupful into a pot. He opened the stove door and blew on the coals to rekindle the fire, then closed the door and put the pot on the stove.

"Place the seeds in the pot, and bring me a bowl," the doctor told Lizzie, and she did so.

The wine boiled quickly, and once it had, they waited for the wine-and-seed mixture to cool. It smelled foul. The doctor finally poured it into a mug and brought it to Minka.

"A little tea," she said in her singsong melon-colored voice. She helped Minka to rise a little and swallow some of the concoction. Minka coughed and retched, then vomited into a bowl the doctor held up.

Mother disposed of the bowl while Lizzie bathed Minka's pale face. The veins beat violet on her eyelids. But her breathing was stronger, and her lashes trembled on her cheeks, as if her eyes wanted to open.

"Will that help?" Lizzie asked.

"I hope so," the doctor replied. "I'll come back tomorrow, but send for me if she worsens."

The rest of the day passed quietly. Father went out to the fields, and Lizzie stayed behind to tend the garden, ducking inside often to check on Minka. By late afternoon, Mother was at her own chores, and Minka slept quietly, Marek the cat curled at her feet.

As Lizzie was frying zucchini cakes and stirring borscht for supper, she heard a little cry from Mother, who sat knitting beside Minka. Her heart sinking, Lizzie hurried to the sofa—and there was

Minka, struggling to rise, wan but awake. Mother urged her to lie down again, but Minka insisted on sitting up.

"That smells so good, Lizzie," she said, her voice raspy from disuse. "I feel like I haven't eaten in days!"

"Because you haven't," Lizzie said. She breathed a great, quiet sigh of relief and smiled at her sister. "But you hate zucchini cakes!"

"I like yours," Minka said, which was a lie. "But not when they're on fire."

"Oh!" Lizzie spun and ran to the stove, where her fritters had turned black and were smoking. She snatched the pan off the stove and waved the smoke out the window, coughing. "I'll have more for you in a minute. No fear that we'll run out of zucchini anytime this century!"

And the best sound in the world was Minka's weak, rose-tinted laughter.

CHAPTER 4

Minka didn't really seem to get better, though. She was frail, too feeble to stand. She didn't touch her paints. She couldn't bear to eat anything but zucchini fritters, which Lizzie made for her until she feared the smell of frying squash would make her sick. Deep purple shadows ringed Minka's eyes. She wore one of Mother's kerchiefs wrapped around her head, as much for warmth as to hide her patchy scalp. She was always cold. Even in the summer heat, her hands and feet were like ice, and she shivered whenever the quilt slipped off her shoulders.

Dr. Śmigly came back on Thursday. She examined Minka, then spoke quietly to Mother. Lizzie eavesdropped.

"I'm not pleased with her progress," the doctor said.

"That's because there isn't any progress," Lizzie interjected. Her mother frowned, but the doctor nodded.

"She isn't worse, but she surely is no better. I'll go into town on Monday for some herbs that I think might be helpful. Some feverfew, some milk thistle."

"No need to wait that long. I'll be taking the produce to market tomorrow," Mother said. "I can buy whatever you need then."

"No!" Minka cried out from the sofa, eavesdropping, too. "I will go to market!"

"Minka, you can't," Mother said, and the doctor agreed.

"You're far too weak, child. It could be the death of you." The word *death* hung in the air, a puff of light orange that made Lizzie shiver.

"I will!" Minka insisted. "I must! You can't stop me—you can't!"

She thrashed on the sofa, struggling to rise—and then, amazingly, she managed it. Mother and Lizzie ran toward her, but they were too slow. Minka's legs, weak as a newborn goat's, wobbled under her, and she sank to the wide planks of the floor.

Mother and Dr. Śmigly lifted her gently and helped her back onto the sofa. Lizzie wrapped the quilt around her and hugged her fiercely. Minka's eyes went wide with surprise: Lizzie never hugged.

"I'll go," Lizzie whispered into her sister's ear. "I'll do whatever you want. I'll get whatever you need. Tell me tonight."

Minka nodded. Gradually, she relaxed in Lizzie's arms, and by the time the doctor took her leave, she was asleep.

"I'll go to market," Lizzie declared. Mother's face showed her astonishment, and with an effort, Lizzie raised her gaze to meet Mother's eyes. "I can do it," she said.

"It would be easier...." Mother said uncertainly. "I don't want to leave Minka. But you would have to sell the vegetables and the bread. You'd have to... well, talk to people. Take their money. Give them change. Be–"

"Be nice," Lizzie finished. "I can be nice if I want to. And I'm better at sums than anyone else in school." She wasn't actually certain she could be nice to customers, or even look them in the eye. But she knew she had to go. Something had happened to Minka there, and she needed to find out what it was.

"All right," Mother said. "If you're sure." Lizzie nodded but didn't answer. To say she was sure would have been a lie.

Lizzie helped Minka change into a fresh night-dress before bed, so they could speak privately. It was hard for Minka to talk.

"Find Emil," Minka murmured. "He will give you fruit for me. Tell him I'm ill, but that I'll be there next week. And that I will go with him."

"Go? Go where?"

"With him. To his house. He said I could work there, as an artist. That I could paint, and paint...do nothing but paint."

"What?" Lizzie was dumbfounded. "Go with him? Paint? What are you talking about? You want to be a teacher!"

"No..." Minka said. The words came out slowly, like rose-tinted honey. "No. That's what I *could* do. Not what I want to do. I love painting. I feel... like myself when I paint. But how can a person be a painter here? There's nothing but farms and a few shops. And the market. There's nothing. Emil promised me...everything."

"But..." Lizzie didn't know what to say. She knew Minka loved to paint, but her sister had never told her that was what she wanted to do with her life. They had a plan. They would stay on the farm, and Liz-zie would tend the fields, and Minka would teach the children at the little schoolhouse when their teacher retired. "But you don't need Emil to be a painter! You could—you could paint here, and sell your work at the market."

"Oh, Lizzie," Minka murmured. "No one there would buy. And I must make money to help Mother and Father. They work so hard...." Her voice trailed off, and she was asleep again.

Lizzie barely slept herself that night. She worried about Minka. She worried about going to market. Her worries marched around in her head, a tiny army of waspy thoughts, stinging her awake every time her eyes began to close. *Everyone will be staring at you,* they said, jabbing and piercing. *You won't sell a thing. Minka will get worse while you're gone. There won't be any sign of beautiful Emil with his beautiful fruit.* Or, even worse, *You'll find Emil. And he will ...*

...what? Make her own hair fall out? Lizzie couldn't even imagine.

※

In the morning her eyes felt like sandpaper, and her head ached. She was silent as Mother loaded the vegetables and bread into the wagon. Because Lizzie had taken Minka's chore of helping with the breadmaking, the loaves were lopsided and some were overbaked. Lizzie feared no one would want them.

Mother helped her hitch up Kosmy. The donkey looked at her doubtfully over his shoulder as if to say, "You? I want the other one."

"Me too," Lizzie murmured to him, patting his shoulder. He snorted.

When everything was ready, Lizzie ran inside to say goodbye to Minka. Minka's eyes were brighter, but the shadows under them were just as deep.

"Don't forget," she whispered to Lizzie, clutching at her hand. Lizzie nodded. "Bring me fruit. It will make me feel better. And tell him to wait for me. Tell him I–" She broke off abruptly and coughed.

Lizzie bit her lip. "I'll do what I can," she said. She liked that statement. It promised nothing, really. She patted Minka's hand and went back out, taking Kosmy's reins in her hand and starting down the lane.

When the wagon reached the curve in the lane where Minka always stopped to wave, Lizzie looked behind her. There was the cottage, looking cozy and trim, its thatched roof neat. The paintings Minka had done on the whitewashed walls were vivid and cheerful. It looked so homey, so inviting, and Lizzie wanted so badly to turn around and go back.

But she couldn't. Instead, she tugged on the reins, and Kosmy clip-clopped around the bend.

Lizzie's dread made the trip to Elza seem far longer than it was. She tried to concentrate on the lemon-bright song of a thrush, the silvery rustle of leaves in the breeze. But the fluttering colors made her stumble over her own feet, and they clashed with her thoughts, which were dark and anxious.

At last she could see the half-timbered buildings of town in the distance. The lane from the east joined with hers, and another wagon rumbled toward her. Lizzie stared at the ground.

"Is that . . . Elzbieta?" called a man's voice. "Halloo there, child!"

Lizzie glanced up. The man leading his horse-drawn wagon wore a long beard and a broad smile. She knew him; he was a friend of Father's. He came every year to help with the grain harvest, and Father went to help him in turn. Master Mikolaj, that was his name.

"How's your pa?" Master Mikolaj boomed in a great wave of hunter green. "And where's your big sister? We're not used to seeing you round here!"

"Father's fine. Minka's sick," Lizzie said, her voice low. She always got quieter when other people were loud.

"Sick, eh?" Master Mikolaj shook his head. "Must be that fever that's going around. Here, follow me, girl. I'll show you where Minka usually sets up."

Master Mikolaj pulled his wagon ahead of Lizzie's, and she followed him, grateful both for his help and for the fact that he didn't seem to care if she spoke or not. He kept up a running commentary as they moved into the town, pointing out who lived in which house, what each person did for a living, whether they were a friend or not. He told stories about the emperor and empress and the time they'd visited Elza, back when he was a boy. He described the latest meeting of the town council and what every single councilperson had said about every matter under discussion. Lizzie's head spun with all the names and details.

The dirt lane became cobblestones, and on both sides were shops and even more homes. At last they came to the town green, where the market was set up. On one side was the Town Hall, its roof crowned as always with a storks' nest, wooden scaffolding climbing up its sides. Master Mikolaj had reported that the town council was repairing and redecorating the building. Across the green was the church, its wood-shingled walls rising in the front to a tower topped with a cross. Mother and Father and Minka went to church once in a while, but Lizzie didn't go with them. She'd snuck inside a time or two, though. She'd loved the rich smell of incense and the painted walls and ceiling; the candelabra that hung over the altar; the portraits of saints that worshippers had decorated with fresh flowers. It was a tranquil, beautiful place—when nobody else was there.

Now, though, all the town seemed to be in the square for the market. Tables ringed the green, and it rang with voices that made Lizzie a little woozy as their cacophonous colors rose and mingled in the warm air.

"Your sister takes a place right at the front, here," Master Mikolaj said. "That way, the buyers see her first. It's why she always sells out—that and your delicious bread! Oh, she's a great salesperson, that one. She just lets fly with one of her smiles and *ho!* Everyone buys. That's all you have to do, my girl, smile and be friendly. And have the best bread, of course!" He laughed heartily at his own joke, and Lizzie ventured a small smile. She stopped Kosmy at the spot Master

Mikolaj pointed to, and he helped her unload the little wooden table with folding legs that Father had fashioned.

Master Mikolaj went on to unload his own goods a little distance away, and Lizzie began to pile up the vegetables and bread on the table. She stared determinedly at the red globes of tomatoes and the long braided loaves as she worked, feeling the glances of her neighbors, certain they were whispering about her among themselves.

"Want some help, child?" The woman from the table next to her stood up with a saffron-yellow grunt from her perch on an overturned wooden box. "You must· be Minka's sister, eh? She's told us all about you."

She had? What had she told? Did Minka tell tales of her oddness? Lizzie tried to breathe as slowly as she could, but she could feel panic rising.

"She says you're a good worker, that you help your pa in the fields," the woman went on, pulling squashes from Lizzie's wagon and arranging them in pyramids that looked as though they would roll right off the table. They didn't, though. "And that you're a whiz with the laundry. You can come and do mine anytime!" She let loose with a loud hoot of laughter, and, startled, Lizzie looked up at her. Her frizzy gray hair was escaping on all sides from her kerchief, and her brown eyes were friendly in their nest of wrinkles. Ah–this must be Mistress Klara. Minka had told Lizzie about her, now that she thought of it–nice things. Just like the things she'd told Mistress Klara about Lizzie.

"Thank you," Lizzie managed. She tried to copy Mistress Klara's squash pyramid, scowling as the vegetables rolled away under her fingers.

"Like this," Mistress Klara advised, making a squash triangle at the bottom and then adding vegetables atop it. "I always think they look tastier like that. Not that I'd care if I never saw another squash! But I say that every summer."

"Me too," Lizzie said. She was rewarded by Mistress Klara's bright smile.

"Isn't it silly? In the dead of winter, with the snow two feet deep, I'll be dreaming of sautéed squash–but will I have any? No indeed. I'll have to wait months for it. And then there will be too much, and I won't want a bite. We're never satisfied, we humans!"

Lizzie considered this. It seemed to be true of Minka, but not of her. She was satisfied with her family, the farm, her life. Why weren't other people?

Mistress Klara passed Lizzie a wooden box to sit on, and Lizzie perched, looking up from under her hair at the passersby every now and then. Mistress Klara, realizing at once that Lizzie wasn't going to hawk her goods the way Minka did, took on the job herself, advertising Lizzie's as well as her own.

"Here, good people, are the sweetest squashes, the crustiest breads, the most vine-ripe tomatoes and the greenest green beans you've ever seen!" she called out in a lilting yellow voice that enticed shopper after shopper. Even Lizzie's mouth watered. "You'll be eating well if you buy our wares! Fry a little of my garlic in oil and add the chopped tomatoes, the beans, the squash! Sop up the juices with a rye loaf!"

A group of boys and girls came by. They didn't go to her school, but they seemed familiar. Lizzie looked down quickly, her hair shadowing her face, but not before one of them, a boy, noticed her.

"It's the girl from the dance!" he cried, poking one of his friends. "Remember, Pawel? She had a fit in the Hall!" The friend, Pawel, grinned—then spun around, raised his hands in the air, wailed like a banshee, and fell to the ground writhing. He was mocking her.

It had been two years ago. People came from all the farms and villages around Elza, dressed in their finest, to the harvest dance at the Town Hall. The women wore brightly beaded and embroidered vests with flowered skirts, their lace underskirts peeking out at the bottom. The men were in starched white shirts and vests with tassels, red scarves cinching the waists of their striped pants. The Hall had been decorated with ribbons and streamers and lighted with candles. There were refreshments—ale and ice cider and fruit kompot, raspberry-filled pączki and dumplings, slices of babka and candies. Mother had brought her special poppy seed cookies. The floor of the ballroom was polished as smooth as a mirror, and at one end a band tuned up on a dais, testing their fiddles and accordions.

Lizzie hadn't wanted to go. She begged to stay home alone, but Mother said she was too young. And Minka had been so desperate to attend her first dance: Mother had even embroidered a new vest for her, blue velvet with red flowers and gilt beading the exact color of Minka's hair. She looked wonderful in it, her golden locks twisted overnight in rags so they cascaded down her back in thick spirals, a flower circlet on her head. Lizzie couldn't bear to keep her sister from going, from being the loveliest girl there, from dancing with all the boys. When Minka took her aside and said, "It won't be so very bad! And don't worry. I'll be right there with you," she knew she had to go. So she dressed in her own best vest and an old skirt from the year before, its hem let down so it reached her ankles.

Her dread grew as they neared Elza. By the time they'd settled Kosmy with the other donkeys and wagons outside the Hall, she was nauseated and trembling. But still, for Minka, she placed one foot after the other and let her too-tight shoes carry her inside.

It was hot in the Hall, airless and crowded. The smells of perfumes and overheated bodies mingled with the scents of the baked goods on the long tables under the windows. The colors of voices chattering, greeting and gossiping, rose and blended in the air until they were nothing but a cloud of muddy brown. Minka ran off immediately to join a group of friends, and Lizzie crept to a corner, where she hunched, pressing herself into the wall.

It was when the musicians began to play that things fell apart. Lizzie had never heard more than one musical instrument playing at a time. Each fiddle produced a different shade of blue—robin's-egg, royal, periwinkle. If that wasn't enough, other instruments joined in, bright orange horns and oxblood drums and a hurdy-gurdy squealing garish green. The noise was overwhelming, cacophonous. Lizzie squeezed her eyes shut and pressed her hands to her ears, but she was unable to silence the din. She couldn't make out a tune, only a blast of noise and, every time she opened her eyes, wild, swirling colors that grew louder and brighter, louder and brighter, until she added her own voice to it, screaming and screaming, rolling on the floor in an attempt to shut it all out.

Minka had rushed to her, held her, dragged her out of the Hall and into the quiet of the night. She'd sat with Lizzie until she stopped shaking; helped her into the wagon; convinced Mother and Father to take them home. She never once—then or later—blamed or criticized Lizzie for the ruined evening. But Lizzie could barely stand to remember it: the nightmarish rush of voices and music and colors that threatened to choke her, the utter terror. The horrible guilt for having spoiled Minka's first dance.

Now, the children laughed at the memory of Lizzie's breakdown—all except for one girl who kicked at Pawel and said, "Don't be such an idiot, Pawel." Mistress Klara shot up, knocking over her box-chair, and started to come around her table toward them. All five of them rushed away, Pawel scrambling to his feet to catch up with the others and escape the wrath that was Mistress Klara.

"Troublemakers!" Mistress Klara huffed, settling herself back on her box. "The players at that dance were terrible—I remember it well. Couldn't keep to the rhythm at all. I'd have shouted them down, too, if I'd thought of it!" Lizzie understood that she was trying to be nice, but Mistress Klara's words—the knowledge that she'd been there, too, and seen it all—just added to her humiliation. The urge to flee was overwhelming, and she stood up.

"That's right, child, you walk around and see what's offered," Mistress Klara said. Her voice was gentle. "I'll mind your table. Take your time."

Lizzie was too distressed to thank her. She simply stumbled away from the square and into the streets of Elza. It was quiet away from the market. Most of the shops were closed, as their owners were selling their wares in the square, or buying goods there themselves. Houses stood silent, their windows open to the warm summer air, and an occasional dog looked up panting from a stoop, too hot to do more than cock an ear at her passing.

Gradually her breathing calmed, and she started

back. She had a job to do—for Minka, as well as for Mother and Father. She needed to find Emil.

She had to search the market. So she walked slowly around the square, wondering where Emil and his people might have their fruit stand. She stopped briefly at a stall selling herbs, buying feverfew and milk thistle for Dr. Śmigly. She didn't look at the seller; she didn't even know if it was a man or a woman. She just passed over her coppers and took the change.

She continued on, almost to the far side of the square now. There were so many stalls! A table of old shoes, some without mates; hutches of rabbits; a stand holding wobbly stacks of old books and chipped bowls.

To the side of the shoe stand was a plum tree in bloom, its boughs heavy with dark pink blossoms. Below, in its shade, Lizzie saw a long, low table made of some dark burnished wood, piled high with glistening fruits.

There were apples in every shade of red imaginable—crimson, ruby, scarlet, vermillion. Lizzie knew all the names of those colors from Minka's paints, but she had only seen them truly in sounds. Yet here they were in apples, all different sizes—and all of them perfect. Beside them were grapes, green and red and purple; apricots at the height of ripeness; plump cherries. There were plums so darkly purple they were nearly black, and velvet-napped peaches that looked as delicious as they probably tasted. There were strange scaly fruits with what looked like little trees atop them. There was every kind of berry Lizzie could imagine, as well as many she couldn't identify—all ripe at the same time.

And behind the table, which looked far too heavy to have been carried to market, was a boy.

Lizzie didn't usually think of people as attractive or unattractive. She knew Minka thought Jakob was nice-looking, but she just saw his brown curls and funny smile and the scar on his temple. Everyone said Zofia was pretty, but Lizzie knew how mean she was, and so she noticed only the twist of her lip when she spoke. When Lizzie looked in the mirror herself, she saw the streak of dirt on her neck or the way her straw-colored hair needed brushing, not a person who was pretty or ugly. She had no idea what she looked like to other people.

But it was impossible not to notice that this boy was beautiful. His skin was flawless, creamy; his wild black curls lay just so, despite their unruliness. He was tall and lean and held himself with a confidence that the boys Lizzie knew didn't have. Clearly this was Minka's Emil. And when Lizzie forced herself to raise her gaze to his tawny eyes, he was looking straight at her, a little smile playing on his perfect mouth.

Startled, Lizzie backed away, almost tripping on a loose cobblestone. The boy grinned, showing teeth as white as bone.

"Lizzie!" he called, beckoning to her. "Come and taste the fruit! It's especially good today—you must take some home to your sister!"

As shocking as it was that he knew her name, that he knew she was Minka's sister, there was something far more disturbing to Lizzie about his words.

They had no color at all.

CHAPTER 5

Lizzie forced herself to walk up to the table. Emil stood alone on the other side, arranging fruit on a heavy golden dish. He held out a peach. "Taste it," he said. "You'll never eat anything better."

"No, thank you," Lizzie answered. It was so strange to her that her vision stayed clear when he spoke, that the air didn't tremble with a wash or a cloud or a swirl of color. This had never happened before.

"No?" Emil said. "Are you sure? Certain? Definite? Look at it. It's perfect."

The peach *was* perfect. It held every hue of orange and pink on its blushing skin; it was so ripe it looked like it was about to burst. Lizzie could smell it from across the table, its sweetness begging her to take a bite.

"No," she said again, looking away. But she was

hungry. She had been too nervous to eat breakfast. Her stomach rumbled, and Emil's smile grew broader.

"A plum, then?" he suggested. "No, try an apple. You've never tasted this one, I'm sure—the Bloody Ploughman." He picked up a dark red apple that glinted in the sun and tossed it from hand to hand. "Want to know how it got its name?"

Lizzie was silent.

"There was a ploughman caught stealing apples from his lord's orchard, and the guards shot him dead. His grieving wife took his bag of plunder and tossed it on the trash heap, weeping, and where the apples and her tears fell, a tree grew. And it produced these." He bit into the apple with his white teeth, and the crunch of it made Lizzie shudder.

"Take one to your sister," Emil urged. "Take a bag full of fruit. Minka needs it. It will give her strength."

Lizzie summoned up all her courage. "How do you know who I am?" she demanded.

Emil laughed. "I'd know you anywhere," he said. "My lovely Minka described you perfectly. Pretty and shy, strange and fearful—that's what she said. A devoted sister, a special girl. I knew you as soon as I saw you."

Pretty, shy, strange, fearful—was that what Minka saw when she looked at Lizzie? Lizzie shook her head. Minka knew there was more to her than that ... or maybe not. After all, Lizzie hadn't known that Minka wanted to be an artist. Maybe they *didn't* know everything about each other.

"What did you promise her?" Lizzie asked in a low voice.

"Why, her heart's desire, of course," Emil said. "How could I do anything else? Your sister has my love. I would do anything to make her happy."

Lizzie looked straight at him then, trying to see if he meant it. He met her gaze squarely. But she could see nothing in his eyes. There were no depths to them. If he truly loved Minka, it didn't show.

"I don't like you," Lizzie said bluntly. "And I don't want your fruit. It's made Minka sick, and I don't want her to eat any more of it."

Emil's dark brows drew together, and his smile faded. "Not so fearful after all, are you?" he said. "So Minka had it wrong. How sad, when sisters don't truly know each other."

Lizzie backed away. "We do know each other. We do!" she protested. "But we don't know you. And we don't want to. Stay away from Minka."

"Oh, I will stay away—if she wants me to," Emil promised. "But she won't want me to. Neither will you, later."

It sounded like a threat, coming colorless from his perfect mouth. Lizzie scowled. She didn't want him to see that he frightened her.

"If you won't bring your sister any fruit," Emil said, "I do hope you will agree to give her this little bauble. I bought it right here, at the market. It reminded me of her."

He pushed a small wooden box across the table, and Lizzie picked it up.

"Open it," Emil urged. The box was hinged at the top, and Lizzie opened the lid. Inside, nestled in cotton, was a silver pendant in the shape of a flower, inlaid with pink stones. It was charming and pretty, and it reminded Lizzie, too, of Minka. It annoyed her that she and Emil agreed on something.

"I don't think you should be giving Minka presents," she said. "You hardly know each other."

"It's nothing," Emil said. "A trinket. A trifle. Promise me you will give it to her. Promise."

Lizzie frowned. She didn't trust Emil—but she knew how delighted Minka would be with the gift. It might be just what she needed to help her get better.

"All right," she said reluctantly. "I'll give it to her."

"Good! Oh, good girl!" Emil exclaimed. "What a dear, devoted sister!" He clapped his hands together, and the colorless sound of it made Lizzie turn, pick up her skirts, and run back toward her own table.

Behind her she could hear Emil laughing.

The church bells were striking five and Mistress Klara was packing up as she arrived. Her round face creased in concern when she saw Lizzie. "You're pale as parchment!" she cried. "Are those children giving you more trouble?"

Lizzie counted her breaths, making each one slower and deeper than the one before. Gradually her legs stopped trembling. "I'm all right," she managed. "Oh—the breads are all sold!" There were still zucchinis left on her table, but every merchant was selling those; she hadn't expected them to go.

"I took the payments," Mistress Klara said. "Here you are." She handed a pouch of coins to Lizzie.

"Thank you," Lizzie said. How nice Mistress Klara was! "Let me help you. You've done so much for me."

"You can put the boxes in my cart," Mistress Klara said. "They're a bit heavy for this old back."

As Lizzie hefted the wooden boxes, mostly empty,

into Mistress Klara's cart, she asked, "Do you know someone named Emil? A fruit seller?"

"Emil?" Mistress Klara mused. "I used to know an Emil who came here, but he sold carved pieces. Ducks and rabbits mostly, but he'd make something on request if you asked. He was a whiz with a whittling knife. He passed on, though, awhile back. At the age of eighty-three."

"This one is young. And…handsome."

"Oho!" Mistress Klara crowed. "I see. A handsome boy, selling ripe fruits. How interesting!"

Lizzie looked down at her feet. "He's a friend of Minka's," she muttered.

"Ah," Mistress Klara said. "Yes, the boys like Minka, don't they? But it will be your turn soon enough, don't you worry." Her smile was kind.

"I'm not worried," Lizzie said, and Mistress Klara laughed.

"Good! Plenty of time for that."

The carts loaded and donkeys hitched, Mistress Klara reached out to hug Lizzie goodbye. Lizzie ducked away.

"Thank you again for your help," she said formally.

Mistress Klara shook her head. "You're a funny

little thing, aren't you? Well, you are very welcome indeed. I hope you'll come again next week, and we can get to know each other a little better. I'm sure Minka will be well by then, but you must come anyway, and keep us company. It wasn't so bad, was it?"

Lizzie wasn't sure how to respond. It hadn't been terrible, except for the teasing children. And Emil. The rest—well, it had been interesting. But her nerves were jangled, and she knew she wouldn't be able to calm down enough to sleep well that night. So she just gave Mistress Klara a half smile and a wave, and headed toward the town gate in the direction of home.

It was cool under the thick leaves of the overhanging trees, and Kosmy trotted with more than his usual energy. He wanted his supper. Lizzie was famished, too. When the cottage came in sight, Kosmy picked up speed, and Lizzie matched his pace. Minka stood in the doorway, propped against the frame. She raised her arm in a weak hello and took a step toward Lizzie, then wobbled. Lizzie dropped the reins and hurried to her sister.

"You should be lying down!" she scolded, but Minka ignored her words.

"Tell me," she begged. "Did you see him? What did he say?"

Lizzie frowned. "I'll be in soon. I have to feed Kosmy. Go lie down."

"Tell me now! Kosmy can wait!" Minka stamped her foot, and Lizzie stared at her, surprised.

Didn't she care that Kosmy was tired after his day's work? Minka always fed him as soon as she got back from market. The donkey was her pet, nuzzling her pockets for treats, following her around like a dog. He expected special treatment. Now he stood confused, reins hanging, looking mournful and hungry.

But the foot-stamp was too much for Minka, and she swayed like a willow branch. Lizzie grabbed her elbow and helped her inside. "I'll feed you in a few minutes," she called over her shoulder to Kosmy, and he snorted with displeasure.

"You're back!" Mother was stirring a big pot on the cast-iron stove. Lovely smells rose up from it. "How did it go? Did you sell much?"

"She'll tell you at supper!" Minka pulled Lizzie to the sofa and sat close.

"Tell me everything," she said, her voice low. "Did you see him?"

Lizzie nodded.

"Oh, hurrah! Isn't he wonderful? Isn't he kind? What did he say?"

Lizzie looked over at her mother, but she was busy chopping herbs.

"He was very—well, odd, Minka. He wanted me to try his fruit, and he kept insisting. And he said things—strange things."

Something flashed in Minka's eyes that Lizzie had never seen before. "He wanted you to eat his fruit? *You?*"

Lizzie nodded again.

"And did you eat?" Minka's tone was almost fierce.

"No. He scared me."

Minka laughed in relief. "Scared you? Lizzie, you're scared of everything. Emil isn't the least bit scary. What did he say about me?"

Lizzie thought back. She wanted to lie but couldn't. "He said you were lovely. He said...he said you had his love."

Minka sank back on the cushions, a small smile on her lips. "Oh, Lizzie," she sighed.

"And then," Lizzie said, low, "he—well, he threatened us. You and me."

Minka drew her brows together. "Why, that's absurd! He would never. What did he say? I'm sure you misunderstood."

Lizzie tried to remember. She had told him to stay away from Minka—but she couldn't tell her sister that. And he'd replied, *But she won't want me to. Neither will you, later.* That had sounded menacing at the time, but was it really? Maybe she was wrong. She was so often wrong about people.

"It was nothing," she said to Minka. "You're right, I misunderstood."

"Did he give you anything for me? A–a gift, perhaps?"

Lizzie blinked. "Why—yes. How did you know?"

Minka sat up again. "What did you bring?" she asked eagerly. "Is it fruit?"

"It's just a–a bauble, he said. A trinket."

Minka looked crestfallen for a moment. Then she held out her hand. "Well, let me see!"

"You shouldn't be taking presents from him," Lizzie said.

"Give it to me!" Minka cried, and Mother turned from her cooking.

"Shh," Lizzie warned.

Minka looked up at Lizzie through her eyelashes. "I'm *sure* his gift will make me feel better," she said, low. "I do feel so poorly, Lizzie." Lizzie saw how exhausted she looked, how pathetic with her limp gray hair peeking out from her kerchief.

"Here, then," Lizzie said reluctantly. She pulled the little box out of her pocket. Minka sprang at her and grabbed for it. "Minka!"

Minka's fingers closed around the box. She wrenched it away and opened it violently, breaking the top off. Then she pulled out the pendant, holding it close to her face, turning it this way and that.

"Ah," she said. "It's a locket!" Lizzie hadn't noticed that it was hinged. Minka opened it, and something fell out onto her lap. Lizzie and Minka both shot out their hands for it, but Lizzie was faster.

It was a cherry, the smallest, most perfect cherry Lizzie had ever seen.

She held it to her nose and inhaled deeply. It smelled better than any cherry had ever smelled—like sweetness and sunshine mixed. Gently, testingly, she squeezed it, and a drop of its red juice fell on her other hand. Minka bent down to lick it. Aghast, Lizzie yanked her arm away, dropping the cherry—and Minka seized it and popped it in her mouth. As Lizzie watched, she chewed, and her angry expression smoothed.

"Supper's almost ready, girls," Mother called from the stove.

Minka turned her head to smile. "Lizzie's telling me stories of the market," she said. Lizzie could hardly believe how effortlessly the lie slipped out. "It makes me feel so much better to hear about it! I'm sure I'll be able to go next week."

Mother came over and touched her wrist to Minka's forehead. "You do look better," she agreed. "Can you eat at the table with us?"

"I believe so," Minka said.

"I'll lay a place for you." Mother stroked Minka's kerchief-covered head and went back to the stove.

As soon as she turned her back, Minka closed her eyes and sighed deeply. Lizzie could see her licking her lips, getting every bit of the cherry juice. A faint flush rose up from her neck to her cheeks.

"Marvelous," she whispered. "Oh, Lizzie, you must taste next time! I'm sorry I was mean about sharing."

"I don't think I want to share," Lizzie said quietly.

Minka spat the cherry pit into her palm and held it out. "We should plant it!" she said. "Then we'll always have beautiful cherries of our own. Will you do it?"

Lizzie took the cherry pit and looked at it closely. It looked like any other cherry pit, only smaller. "I'd rather not."

"Please, Lizzie!" Minka pressed. "It made me feel better! You see?"

Lizzie considered. Minka did look better. Perhaps the cherry *had* helped. "Fine," she said finally.

"Do it now," Minka urged. "Oh, first, help me put on the locket!"

"Mother will see it," Lizzie warned. "What will you say if she asks about it?"

Minka thought for a moment. "No, you're right," she agreed. "I'll just put it here, under my pillow." She slid the silver necklace under her pillow on the sofa, and then lay back, smiling dreamily.

Lizzie fed Kosmy quickly, and then looked for a suitable place to plant the cherry pit. There: at the edge of the vegetable garden between the cottage and the stable. It was a sunny spot, too far from the beds to shade the garden plants, but still close enough that Lizzie wouldn't forget to water it. She dug a little hole and put the pit in, then covered it with soil and drizzled water from a cup over it.

But she didn't really want it to grow.

Minka sat at the table and ate with some appetite for the first time in many days, and supper was merry. Father recounted his showdown with a groundhog and Lizzie described the people she'd seen and the selling she'd done. Of course she admitted that Mistress Klara had done most of the work, but Mother and Father were pleased anyway.

"It's very good to know you can do it, Lizzie," Father said. "You're a plucky girl, I've always known. It's far braver to overcome a fear than not to feel fear at all."

Lizzie looked down at the table, elated. It was rare to have a compliment from Father greater than the nods he gave when she'd put in a good day's work with him.

"And next time," Mother added, "you can do the selling yourself, now that Mistress Klara has shown you how."

Next time! Lizzie hoped there wouldn't be a next time. The strain of going to market had left her utterly exhausted.

"I'm sure Minka will be able to go next week," she said.

"Oh, I will," Minka assured her. "But wouldn't it be fun if you came with me?"

Lizzie thought for a moment. "No," she said at last, and Minka, Mother, and Father laughed.

"Trust our Lizzie to tell the truth!" Mother said, shaking her head. But for once it didn't sound like a criticism, and even Lizzie smiled.

In the morning, though, all jolliness was over. Minka would not wake up.

CHAPTER 6

"Minka!"

Lizzie woke to her mother's despairing cry.

"Minka, open your eyes! *Minka!* Oh, Lizzie, help me!"

Lizzie tumbled down the ladder and dashed to the sofa. Minka lay there asleep, a small smile playing on her lips. Mother stood over her, hands to her cheeks. Marek the cat paced on the rug, his tail pointed straight up.

"She won't wake! I can't wake her!"

Lizzie patted her sister on the shoulder, then shook her. Shook her harder. But Minka slept on.

"Is she breathing?" Lizzie could hardly breathe herself. But yes, Minka's chest rose and fell beneath the coverlet.

"Fetch the doctor! And your father!" Mother exclaimed.

Grabbing a shawl and wrapping it over her

nightdress, Lizzie slipped into her boots and ran outside. She hurried to the back field, where Father was sharpening his scythe in preparation for cutting the grain later in the month.

"Father!" she called as she ran. "Come quickly, it's Minka! She won't wake up!"

The scythe fell from Father's hands. He joined Lizzie in her sprint back to the cottage.

"She's alive," Lizzie panted. "She just won't wake. I'm to fetch the doctor."

"Go, child," Father commanded as he ducked inside, the low doorframe knocking his hat to the ground.

Lizzie pounded down the lane, passing only crows and a nervous rabbit this early in the morning. As she neared Dr. Śmigly's house, though, she heard someone call her name.

"Lizzie, what is it? What's wrong?" In his father's field, Jakob stood, shading his eyes from the newly risen sun.

"Can't stop," Lizzie gasped. She ran on to the doctor's and hammered on the front door, which opened immediately. Dr. Śmigly must have seen or heard her coming; she was dressed and carried her bag, and she came out and pulled the door shut behind her.

"Is she—" the doctor began.

"She's alive," Lizzie managed. She thought for a moment she might throw up, she'd run so fast and so far.

"Breathe, child," the doctor commanded, and Lizzie bent nearly double, drawing in air like the great bellows in the blacksmith's shop.

"Is it Minka?" Jakob had come up beside them. He carried a scythe like Father's and wore a broad-brimmed straw hat to shade his face from the sun.

"She won't wake up," Lizzie said when she could finally talk. "We have to hurry!"

"We'll walk quickly," the doctor said. "But no running. If she only sleeps, we have time."

"I'll come, too," Jakob said. "Maybe I can help."

"But your father," Dr. Śmigly protested. "If he finds you shirking—"

"I'm getting too big to beat now," Jakob said calmly. "I'm not afraid of him."

Lizzie doubted this was true. Jakob's father was a terrible person. At threshing time a couple of years earlier, he had come by to help—not because he was generous, but because that was what was done, and he needed the help his neighbors would give him later on. The threshers had disturbed a nest of late rabbit babies, and he'd wrung their necks, one by one. "They won't be eating your fall vegetables, that's for sure!" he'd told Father, whose appalled expression had mirrored Lizzie's. Minka had cried so hard she'd had to go to bed. Lizzie found it hard to believe that anyone could face that man without fear. But she was glad Jakob was with them. He was a comforting presence.

As they strode—nearly running, but not quite—Jakob asked, "Minka is ill, then? Is it the ague? I've heard that Lidia and Wilek were sick with it awhile back."

"No," Lizzie said.

"The whooping cough, then? Or measles?"

"No."

"Well, what then? Is it serious?" Jakob was worried, Lizzie could tell.

"I don't know," she said shortly. "Her...her hair fell out. She sleeps all the time, and she's too weak to go to market. She has no appetite. Today she wouldn't wake up."

Jakob stopped walking, shocked, then jogged to catch up again with Lizzie. "Her *hair* fell out? She won't wake up? What on earth...?"

Lizzie shook her head as the cottage came into view. She broke into a run.

Inside, Mother sat on a stool beside the sofa. Minka lay unmoving, her hands crossed over her chest, corpselike. Lizzie felt a great, dark cry rising inside her, but Father touched her gently on the shoulder as she stood, hand over her mouth.

"There's no change," he said, and Lizzie gasped in relief. "The doctor—?"

"I'm here," Dr. Śmigly said, panting. "Let me see the patient." Quickly she went to Minka's side, and Mother gave up her place. Jakob came in then, looking uncomfortable.

"I hope I'm not intruding," he said, his hat in his hand. Mother and Father barely glanced at him.

Dr. Śmigly examined Minka thoroughly. Then she motioned to Mother, Father, and Lizzie to sit at the table with her.

"She seems only to be sleeping," the doctor said. "I'm afraid I cannot tell you why she won't wake up. Has anything happened that might cause a change in her condition? A sudden shock, bad news—even an unexpected noise?"

Mother shook her head. "Nothing," she said. "She was better yesterday. She ate a little supper with us, and then went to sleep happily. I thought she might awaken well this morning, but..."

"Perhaps it was the food," Dr. Śmigly mused. "If she was not used to eating much, a large meal could have disturbed her equilibrium. It's very possible that this condition will pass." She stood up. "I'll come back tomorrow and see how she is doing. Keep her comfortable, and if she wakes at all, be sure she drinks something."

Lizzie walked the doctor and Jakob back to the lane. Jakob's expression was pinched as he said, "I can't believe how ill she looks. She was perfectly fine less than a fortnight ago! What happened to her? I don't understand it!"

"None of us does," the doctor said, shaking her head. "Lizzie, can you think of anything that might have pushed her into this state? Anything at all?"

Lizzie bowed her head. "She—she ate a cherry," she said. "From the stand at the market, where she got the fruit before."

She could hardly bear it. This was her fault, she knew.

"A single cherry?" Dr. Śmigly asked.

Lizzie nodded. "It made her better at first—it did! But now—"

"We have to find out where this fruit comes from!" Jakob said. "It looks like someone's poisoning her!"

"It was that boy, at the market," Lizzie said. "The one she was talking about a few weeks ago. Emil, his name is. I think she's in love with him."

Jakob took a quick, sharp breath, and his brows drew together. "I'll find him," he vowed. "I'll get him to explain this—to stop it. If he's made her sick, he must know how to cure her."

"Market day isn't till Friday," Lizzie pointed out. "What will happen to her by then? That's almost a week away!"

"She's stable," Dr. Śmigly said. "If we can keep her from declining...but why would this Emil want to harm her? It's all very odd, very..." Her voice trailed off. "Oh, I've left my glasses inside!"

Lizzie sighed. "They're around your neck." The doctor had finally gotten a chain for her glasses. As Lizzie had predicted, it didn't help.

Dr. Śmigly looked down. "So they are," she said. "If they'd been a snake, they would have bitten me! Come, Jakob, walk me back."

"I'll be right there," Jakob said, and the doctor started off down the lane.

Jakob turned to Lizzie. "This boy, Emil—do you know him?"

"I've met him," Lizzie said. "He was at the market yesterday."

"What is he like?"

"I don't like him," Lizzie said firmly. "He's strange and pushy and too sure of himself. I don't think he means well."

Jakob balled up his fists. "I'll kill him," he said, his voice fierce. "If he's responsible for hurting Minka, I'll kill him."

"Don't say that, Jakob!" Lizzie protested. "That's something your father would say!"

The way Jakob's expression changed then told Lizzie that what she'd said was wrong. His face crumpled, and he almost looked as if he would cry.

"I'm sorry–" Lizzie started, but Jakob interrupted her.

"No, you're right," he said. "There's a part of him in me, and I try all the time to keep it from coming out. I don't want to be like him."

"You're *not* like him," Lizzie assured him. "Not one bit. You're kind and funny."

Jakob managed a smile. "Thanks, Lizzie."

"And besides," Lizzie said in a low voice, "if Emil has hurt Minka, I want to kill him, too."

Jakob blinked, surprised. Then he nodded. "All right then," he said. "Listen, if you're going to be nursing Minka, your father will need some help in the fields—I can do that. I'll come back as soon as I'm done with my own work. And if Minka doesn't get better, we'll go to market together, and we'll find this Emil." He patted Lizzie on the shoulder, and she kept herself from flinching, for his touch was warm and sympathetic. Then he started off at a trot after the doctor.

❦

The days passed slowly for Lizzie. There was no change in Minka. She slept on, nearly motionless on the sofa. Mother and Lizzie bathed her and made sure she was warm. They spooned water and soup into her, and she swallowed obediently, eyes closed. Jakob came late in the afternoon nearly every day and spent a few hours helping Father. He stopped by the cottage when he was done, always with a hopeful look on his face. But Minka stayed asleep.

Dr. Śmigly sent a note. She'd been called away on an emergency and would stop by when she returned.

There was no need for her anyway, as far as Lizzie could tell; Minka's condition remained the same.

One afternoon Stefan came with his brother. He wandered into the cottage looking for a snack and stared, fascinated, at Minka lying motionless on the sofa. Her kerchief had fallen off.

"What's wrong with her?" he demanded. "Why does her hair look so strange?"

"She's asleep," Lizzie told him, adjusting the kerchief. She ignored his second question.

"Why doesn't she wake up?"

"I don't know."

"Minka!" Stefan shouted, and Mother jumped at the stove. "Wake up, you!"

"Hush, child," Mother scolded.

"Why?" Stefan asked practically. "Being quiet won't wake her up."

"Out!" Mother commanded, pointing to the door. "This is no laughing matter. Go bring me some tomatoes for the stew." Cowed, Stefan hurried outside. He was back a moment later.

"There's something weird out here," he said. "Come see!"

Lizzie sighed. "Go get the tomatoes, Stefan," she said.

"No, really! Come on, you have to look!" Stefan danced from foot to foot, and Lizzie turned from Minka to follow him outside.

The clouds that had been threatening rain all day had massed in the west, and the sunset colored them with wild streaks of red and orange. Lizzie took a deep breath, inhaling the thick smell of late summer. She looked around. There was nothing unusual. A rabbit lurked beneath a bush, but otherwise only the warning breeze, damp with the coming storm, moved in the yard.

"Stefan—" she began, but he interrupted.

"Look!" He pointed a grubby finger at a small tree by the garden.

Lizzie blinked. Surely there hadn't been a tree there before. And certainly not *this* tree. Stefan was right—it was weird. It was small, no taller than Stefan himself, the bark maroon, the limbs twisted into outlandish shapes, coiled around each other like snakes.

"I planted a cherry pit there," Lizzie said slowly. "Three days ago."

"Well, that can't be it," Stefan said reasonably. "Nothing grows in three days."

"But—this did. It's a cherry tree."

All at once, Lizzie remembered the plum tree

she'd seen the day she met Emil. A plum tree in full bloom in July, when plums bloomed in May. What had Minka said? ... *He took the pit and dug a little hole in the ground and put it in, and he said a plum tree would grow there, and we would always know exactly where we had first met.* If it was the same one, it had grown and blossomed in a week's time—much like this tree.

Marek the cat had followed them outside. He circled the tree, his tail high, hissing.

"What is he doing?" Stefan stepped closer to touch the bloodred bark—and then jumped back with a squeal.

"What?" Lizzie cried. "Did something sting you?"

"Look at it," Stefan said, his voice hushed. "There's... there's a face in it."

Lizzie stepped back and looked again at the tree. Stefan was right.

It looked like there was a face staring out from the trunk of the tree. Whorls of bark were its eyes and nose, and a flat plane of lichen made a grimacing mouth. It was a horrid, nightmarish face.

"It's just the bark," Lizzie said, trying to sound reassuring. Her voice wobbled a little. "It's just a tree."

"We should cut it down."

"I don't know," Lizzie said. "What if it grows cherries? What if they wake Minka up and make her better again, like the cherry she ate?" Though whether that cherry had helped or hurt, Lizzie still wasn't sure. Minka had been better, and then she'd gotten worse. Which was the result of eating the cherry? Had it sent Minka into her sleep, or had it kept her awake one day longer?

Stefan shook his head. "I wouldn't eat anything from that tree. It's nasty. Don't give her any cherries. Cut it down!"

Lizzie looked at the tree again, at its uncanny face. "You're right," she decided. "I will cut it down. I hate it."

"Now?" Stefan said eagerly. He loved axes and knives—anything with a sharp blade.

"Tomorrow," Lizzie said firmly.

"But I want to help," Stefan said, disappointed.

"If I need help doing it, I'll send for you," Lizzie promised. She didn't want him jumping around while she tried to chop down a tree with an axe. Someone would be sure to lose a finger at the very least.

"Come on, let's get the tomatoes," Lizzie said. Stefan followed her to the garden. It was unnerving walking with the tree at her back; it felt like the face was watching her go. *It's just a tree,* she said to herself, but she shivered.

When Jakob came in from the fields, she showed him the strange new tree.

"It's from the cherry that Emil person gave to Minka," she said. "It grew in three days."

"In three days?" Jakob walked around the tree, shaking his head. "I don't understand any of this. And see that?" He pointed to the lichen. "It looks like it has a face."

"Isn't it horrid?" Lizzie agreed. "I'm going to chop it down."

"Good," Jakob said. It almost seemed to Lizzie that the leaves rustled–a sighing, murmuring sound–when Jakob spoke. But the breeze had died; the air was as still as standing water, and she saw no silvery leaf-noise color.

Mother invited the boys to stay for supper, but Jakob rushed them out the door so they could return home before they were missed.

"That man," Mother said, shaking her head as Father came in from the fields to wash up.

"Their father?" Lizzie asked, setting bowls on the table. Only three bowls–it was strange how they'd gotten used to Minka not sitting with them. But at least, Lizzie told herself, she was there. Lying motionless on the sofa, but *there*.

"He always had a mean streak," Father said. "As long as I can remember, he liked a fight."

"But he wasn't always that bad," Mother said. "I remember when we were young—he was a handsome lad. All that red hair! And he loved to dance. He was first on the floor at every town dance."

Lizzie's eyes widened. She couldn't imagine Jakob's father dancing, his heavyset frame graceful on the parquet floor of the Hall, his dirt-crusted fingers clasping the waist of a village girl.

"What happened to him?"

"His wife died, a year or so after Stefan was born," Mother said, bringing the pot of stew to the table. She dished out portions, with one set aside for Minka. Lizzie would feed it to her after it cooled a bit. "He loved her—oh, terribly much. Nothing was too good for her. He would bring her breakfast in bed. Imagine!" She looked sideways at Father, and he hid a smile. "And then she died, and he changed. He grew hard and cold. I suppose he felt he had to, so he could live in the world without her."

"But . . . she was Jakob and Stefan's mother," Lizzie

pointed out. "They lost her, too. It isn't fair that he's so awful to them because of that. It wasn't their fault."

"People aren't always fair," Mother said. "In fact, most of the time they aren't. They let their feelings tell them what to do."

Lizzie mulled this over. It was true, she'd seen it happen enough times. When children mocked her, or when Mother got mad and yelled at her for something that wasn't her fault, or when their teacher, fed up with Stefan's wildness, made the whole class stay in at lunchtime as a punishment.

"I don't do that," she noted. She wasn't boasting, just stating a fact.

"No, you don't," Mother said warmly, and they began to eat.

In the morning, Lizzie found a small axe in the stable and carried it over to the tree. The face in the bark looked as if it were gaping at her, its whorly eyes following her movement. She took a deep breath and raised the axe, then lowered it again, uncertain.

Then she raised it high and brought it down with a resounding *thwack*.

A scream came from inside the cottage, and Lizzie dropped the axe in shock. "Minka!" she cried, and sprinted inside. Mother bent over Minka, who was lying still on the sofa.

"She screamed," Mother said, her voice shaky. "I don't know why. She just screamed."

"Is she all right?" Lizzie was trembling. Her hands hurt from the rebound of the axe.

"There's no change," Mother said, placing a light blanket over Minka's legs. "Nothing. Just a scream. Perhaps...perhaps she had a bad dream."

But Lizzie knew she hadn't.

It was the cherry tree. Somehow, some way, it was the cherry tree.

Lizzie went back outside and stared at the tree. A drop of dark liquid ran down the trunk from the cut her axe had made. She put out a finger to touch it and pulled it back quickly. Her fingertip was not black with pitch, but bloodred. Appalled, she wiped it on the grass, then picked up the axe and started back to the stable with it. Partway there, she turned around to look at the tree.

The lichen lips of its grotesque face seemed to stretch in a ghastly smile.

CHAPTER 7

Too soon, it was Friday.

Market day.

Filled with dread, Lizzie hitched up Kosmy. She and Mother loaded the cart with vegetables and bread. There were fewer squashes this week. Summer was drawing to an end.

"Good luck," Mother said. She looked weary. The wrinkles around her eyes seemed more pronounced, and her hands trembled a little as she laid tomatoes carefully in their boxes.

"Don't worry," Lizzie assured her. "I'll sell it all. Just take care of Minka."

Mother managed a small smile. She stood and waved till the lane curved and Lizzie could no longer see her.

The route seemed even longer than it had last week. As Lizzie passed the Wood, she looked longingly toward its peaceful greenness. What she wouldn't give to spend an hour lying on the cool, fragrant grass, listening to the forest breathe! But today would give her no peace, Lizzie knew. Her mind went round and round. What should she do if she saw Emil? Even worse—or would it be better?—what should she do if he wasn't there? She was so tired, waking over and over in the night and creeping down the ladder to see if Minka had moved or wakened, listening to her breathing. The nights of broken sleep made her feel slow and stupid.

"Lizzie! Wait!" a voice behind her called out, and she turned to see Jakob running toward her, Stefan skipping behind. Kosmy snorted as she pulled him to a halt.

"What are you doing here?" she asked.

Stefan grinned. "We're going to market with you!"

"I told you I'd go," Jakob reminded her.

A rush of relief washed over Lizzie, but she said, "Jakob, what about your father? Surely he hasn't given you permission."

"As long as we're back by afternoon and I work till sundown in the fields, it'll be fine."

"I'm so glad you're here," Lizzie admitted. "I hate the market. I didn't want to go alone."

"I know," Jakob said. He reached out to pat her

shoulder, then drew back his hand quickly. He knew Lizzie's ways.

Lizzie urged Kosmy on, and Stefan skipped beside her. "Can I help you sell stuff?" he asked.

"Of course," Lizzie said. "You can do all the selling if you want." Stefan clapped his hands.

"He's terrible at sums," Jakob warned. "He'll be giving the bread away so he doesn't have to make change."

"How about this: you sell, I'll do the sums," Lizzie proposed.

"It's a deal." Stefan gripped his own hand and shook it up and down. "You don't like to shake hands, so I'm shaking on it for you," he explained, and she laughed.

The sky was darkening with gray clouds as they reached town, and Lizzie could smell the sulfur of lightning in the air. She didn't have time to worry about storms, though. There was Mistress Klara, her face brightening as she saw Lizzie. She held her arms out for a hug, but Stefan declared, "Lizzie doesn't hug. Not ever!"

"Right," Mistress Klara said. "I'll remember that. I'm glad to see you again, darling! And these two lads—Jakob, the last time I talked to you, you were in short pants and both knees were skinned. And look at you now, you handsome thing!"

Jakob reddened and scuffed his boot in the dirt, and Stefan crowed with laughter. "Him, handsome?" he protested. "With that nose? That hair? He's as ugly as mud!"

Mistress Klara reached out and boxed Stefan's ears, and he pulled away, crying, "Ouch! What did you do that for?"

"Don't be mean to your brother," Mistress Klara commanded. "He's your blood, and nothing is more important. And besides, you and he look just alike." Her voice was authoritative, and Stefan looked flustered for a moment.

Then he laughed. "I can say anything I want." But he stayed out of Mistress Klara's reach.

"He must drive you near mad," Mistress Klara said to Jakob as they helped Lizzie unload and set up her goods.

"Oh yes," Jakob agreed. "He's the biggest pest in the world." At that, Stefan leapt onto his brother's back, trying to wrestle him to the ground, but Jakob reached back and easily plucked him off, holding him at arm's length as Stefan kicked and squealed.

"Make yourself useful," Jakob told him. "Run

around to–where did you say this Emil was?" He looked questioningly at Lizzie.

"At the far end of the square. Way over past the fountain."

"Right. Go there, look for a stand of fruit. Lots of weird fruit. Don't say anything to anyone. Just come back and tell us what you find."

Stefan found this interesting. "Fruit? Like that cherry you planted? Did you cut down the tree yet, Lizzie?"

"No," Lizzie admitted.

"Why not?"

Lizzie didn't want to tell him, didn't want to describe the chop and the scream and the dreadful tree-smile, but she couldn't lie. Instead, she dislodged a pyramid of peppers and busied herself picking them up.

Jakob sent Stefan off. "Remember, be quiet! Like a spy."

"A spy?" Stefan liked this. "Oh, I'll be the best spy. You won't even see me, coming or going!"

Lizzie watched him speed off, intrigued to see that he could indeed blend in with the crowd. In a moment he was gone.

While they waited, Jakob sold bread and peppers,

squash and tomatoes, cajoling buyers to stop and pick up the ripe vegetables and to part with their coppers. He was quite good at it, Lizzie noted. Much better than she was—though she knew anyone would be.

"Why didn't you chop down the tree?" he asked her eventually.

"I tried," she said. "I hit it with the axe—and Minka screamed. As if I'd hit her with it."

Jakob stared at her. "Was she hurt?"

"No. She just…screamed. And the tree—I think it bled."

Jakob shook his head. "That doesn't make any sense."

"None of this does," Lizzie pointed out. "I hate it when things don't make sense."

"Me too," Jakob agreed, passing a loaf of bread to a customer and taking her coppers in return.

It wasn't long until Stefan reappeared, his cap pulled low on his face.

"Well?" Lizzie demanded.

"I saw the stand," Stefan reported. "Lots of nice-looking fruit. Some really weird ones, too. I think that boy was sitting under a tree. Someone's going to steal his stuff."

"We'll go and talk to him," Jakob said. "Stef, will

you stay and sell? Mistress Klara can help you make change."

"You could ask me first," Mistress Klara chided him, and Jakob flushed.

"Sorry—would you help him? Just for a few minutes?"

"Get on with you!" Mistress Klara laughed. "I was just teasing, you great lump."

"Great lump!" Stefan repeated. "That's what I'm going to call you from now on."

Jakob made a face, and Lizzie had to smile.

They made their way across the square. She could smell the stand even before she saw it—the odors of fruit just at its peak, peaches and apples and cherries and pears all mixed together in a scent so sweet that it almost made her gag.

"There he is," she said in a low voice to Jakob.

Jakob looked where she was pointing. "Where?"

"Right there, under the plum tree. Standing behind the table."

Jakob gave her a look of utter bewilderment. "Lizzie, there's nothing under the plum tree. Nothing but flowers that've dropped off. And why is that tree blooming in August?"

Lizzie blinked. She could see Emil clearly. He lounged against his wooden table, picking his nails with a sharp little knife. The breeze from the coming storm ruffled his dark curls, and he lifted his eyes to meet Lizzie's. He smiled.

"You can't see him?" Lizzie breathed. "Not at all?"

"There's some kind of magic at work here," Jakob said uneasily. Lizzie had never heard him use that word before. She didn't know if he believed in magic— or even if she did herself. But she could see fear in his face, and she felt the same fear deep in her chest.

"Come with me," she said. "Pretend you see him. If you can't hear him, pretend you can." She started forward before Jakob could protest, and he followed her.

"Lizzie, Lizzie," Emil said as they drew near. "And a friend! How wonderful. Will he buy some fruit? For his little brother, perhaps?"

"How—" Lizzie began, but she broke off. It didn't matter how Emil knew Jakob had a little brother. What mattered was Minka. "No, he doesn't want any fruit—do you, Jakob?"

"No, we have fruit trees of our own," Jakob said. "We've no need of any fruit today."

"Ah, but your trees don't bear fruit like this!" Emil

held up a pear, plump and tinged with red. Lizzie imagined her teeth sinking into its delicate flesh. Her mouth watered, and she looked away.

"Minka is still sick," she said. "I think it's your fault."

"My fault?" Emil's face was a mask of innocence. "Why would I hurt our Minka? Such a lovely girl."

"She's not your Minka," Lizzie said fiercely.

Emil laughed, his small white teeth flashing. "She *believes* she's mine, dearest Lizzie. And that is what matters. She is sick with longing for me."

"She'll never be yours!" Lizzie cried. "Never!"

"No," Jakob added, picking up the cue. "Minka will never be yours. She belongs to herself."

Emil turned his tawny gaze to Jakob, and he laughed again. "Oh dear me, is this a suitor? Does he want our Minka for his own? You silly boy, you will never have her. A dirty, stupid farmer like you? You're mad if you think so."

Lizzie gritted her teeth, but Jakob's face didn't change. He couldn't hear Emil's insults or see his mocking expression.

"He doesn't see or hear me, does he?" Emil said to Lizzie. "How tragic. He will never know how much a fool I think him."

"He's not a fool," Lizzie hissed. "He's smart as anything!"

Jakob narrowed his eyes and stared at the spot where he imagined Emil was. "No, I'm not a fool," he said. "I'm smart enough to know what you are. You're a zdusze."

Lizzie knew she'd heard that word, *zdusze,* before, but she wasn't quite sure what it meant. Emil knew, though. The taunting smile vanished from his face as if it had been erased from a slate. He bared his teeth, and for an instant Lizzie thought she saw something quite different standing in his place.

He moved around the table toward them. "The girl will die," he snarled, his light, musical voice gone. "Unless she comes to me, she will die."

Lizzie staggered backward as he approached. "No," she managed, her throat closing in terror. "Please. Don't kill her. Please!" Jakob backed up with her, his expression baffled. When he heard her words, though, he stopped, planting his feet firmly.

"I can't see you, but I will find you if you hurt Minka," he said, almost conversationally. "And when I find you, I will kill you."

Emil reached out and made a slapping motion in the air with his hand. Jakob flew backward, landing with a thump on the grass. Emil laughed, and through her shock Lizzie realized that his laughter was as colorless as his words.

Jakob reached up to his cheek, where the imprint of Emil's hand showed red.

"You can't see me," Emil said, "but you can feel me!"

Lizzie stood rooted to the ground. "What do you want with my sister?" she whispered.

"I can give her her heart's desire," Emil said. "You want her to be happy, do you not?"

Jakob stood up and put his hand on Lizzie's arm. She flinched but didn't move away. The touch gave her courage.

"You can never make her happy," she said. "And besides, she can't be with you. She can't even get out of bed."

"She will," Emil promised. "She will rise and come to me. You will see." A crack of purplish-blue thunder punctuated his words, and the wind picked up. The vendors nearby began to move quickly, packing up their goods before the storm hit.

"Go," Emil said, making a brushing movement with his hand as if he were wiping dust from his coat.

A gust of wind hit Lizzie and Jakob, and they staggered backward. Emil motioned again, and the plum tree bent–bent!–and scraped Lizzie's hand as she held it up for balance. It was as if the branch were a knife: the skin on her hand opened and bled. This Jakob could see; his eyes widened in shock, and he grabbed Lizzie's other hand and pulled her away.

When they were out of sight of Emil's table, they ran.

Back at the main market, they found Mistress Klara and Stefan packing up the last of the unsold goods. Mistress Klara took one look at Lizzie, dripping blood, and yanked her flowered kerchief off her head.

"Whatever happened to you, child?" she cried, wrapping the cloth around Lizzie's hand.

Lizzie couldn't speak. The sight of her own blood was making her queasy. Another crack of thunder sounded, and Stefan jumped, his hands over his ears.

"And you, Jakob! Have you been fighting?" The handprint on Jakob's cheek showed clear and red against his skin.

"Not exactly," he said, exchanging a look with Lizzie. She knew what he was asking with that look.

Should they tell Mistress Klara what had happened, what they'd seen? Lizzie had promised Minka not to say anything about Emil to their parents, but this was Mistress Klara.

Still, would Mistress Klara—would *anyone*—believe them?

"Have you ever heard of a zdusze?" she asked. Mistress Klara gave her a quizzical look.

"Well, of course I have," she said. "In tales to give children nightmares. They're the forest goblins, the ones who kidnap young girls."

"Ooo, scary!" Stefan said, laughing. "Did a jooshee whack you in the face like Pa does, Jakob?"

Jakob flushed so red that the handprint disappeared. Mistress Klara turned to Stefan, hands on her hips, and made her voice low. "Go load the boxes in our carts, young man."

Cowed, Stefan hurried to obey, and Mistress Klara turned back. "The old folk say they're real, the zduszes," she said. "I'm an old folk, I suppose, but I've never held much with those stories. Surely you aren't saying you've seen one?"

"Maybe we have," Lizzie said. "I saw him, anyway. Jakob couldn't. But he hit Jakob and knocked him down."

"Jakob couldn't see him?"

"No. He was standing right there, clear as day. But Jakob couldn't see him or hear him at all."

Mistress Klara frowned. "There are always rumors about zduszes and girls gone missing," she murmured. "Every village has a story like that. But I've not heard such a tale here, not that I can recall."

"There was Janina," Lizzie said.

"Janina..." Mistress Klara thought for a moment. "That's right, the girl from Budaro. But she didn't disappear, did she? She was ill and died, or so I recall."

Lizzie nodded. "Yes, that's what Dr. Śmigly said. But I think it might have been goblins. I think they hurt her, or poisoned her with their fruit. And this Emil, he's done the same thing. I think he wants Minka."

Mistress Klara raised an eyebrow skeptically. "But why would you think so, child?"

Lizzie described Minka's sickness and Janina's. "No one knows why either one got sick," she said. "But I know Minka's illness started after she met Emil—the goblin. After she ate his fruit. And—she gave him a lock of her hair."

Mistress Klara's eyes widened. "I don't know

what to think, my dear. A zdusze? It's like saying storybooks are real. Why, it sounds quite mad!"

"People have said that about me before," Lizzie pointed out. "I don't care. I know what I saw. And I know Minka's in danger."

"And I know what I felt," Jakob added, touching his cheek. "I couldn't see him, Mistress Klara, not at all. Lizzie could, but not me. Does that sound normal?"

"Can't say that it does," Mistress Klara admitted. "I'll ask around, see if anyone knows anything. It'll give the old folk something to chatter about, at least."

"Don't say it's about Minka," Lizzie begged. "People will... oh, I don't even know! They'll treat her like a sideshow. She'd hate that!"

"I won't tell," Mistress Klara promised. "I'll just ask. And we can talk next market day."

The wind gusted with a fulvous-colored roar, and enormous drops of rain began to fall. They raised little bursts of dust as they hit the ground, but as they came faster and faster, the dust turned to mud.

"We'd best hurry home or we'll be mired in the mud!" Mistress Klara almost had to shout to be heard over the wind. The rain fell even more fiercely, and in less than a minute Lizzie was drenched. She and Jakob hitched up Kosmy, who looked at them with disgust for forcing him to be out in such weather. Then they slogged back up the lane in a line of other wagons, all hurrying homeward in the sudden storm.

CHAPTER 8

The trip home was nightmarish for Lizzie. Each thunderclap made her gasp and tremble. A tree fell near their wagon, and the dark maroon sound of it nearly undid her. But Jakob kept up a patter of conversation, sensing her panic, and though she couldn't pay attention to his words, their amber regularity helped her steady herself.

And when they reached the cottage at last, Lizzie forgot her terror. Minka was standing in the doorway, just out of the rain, her cheeks as pink as the embroidered flowers in the scarf she had tied around her head.

"You're awake!" Lizzie cried.

Minka laughed at Lizzie's shocked face. "So I am!"

"Why, look at you!" Jakob said. "You look so well. How did this happen? Last time I saw you…"

Minka motioned them inside. "I just…woke up. Not long ago. It was as if I'd had the longest, most delicious sleep. And oh, the dreams! So strange, so wonderful…though some of them were scary. But I've been full of energy, and starving—I haven't stopped eating since I opened my eyes. I could hardly believe it when Mother told me how long I'd been ill. It must have been a terrible sickness—I hope no one else has gotten it!"

In the chaos of the thunderstorm, Lizzie hadn't been able to think about meeting Emil at the market. But now she remembered. And she recalled what he'd said about Minka: *She will rise and come to me.*

Lizzie looked at Jakob. She knew he was thinking the same thing she was: Minka didn't have to worry about anyone else falling ill. No one else would come down with what had ailed her…unless Emil wanted them to.

"I'm so glad you're better," Jakob said. "I was worried."

"Were you?" Minka smiled. "That's very sweet."

Stefan snorted, and Jakob yanked him back out into the downpour to stable Kosmy. As soon as they had gone, Minka turned to Lizzie.

"Did you see him again? Tell me!"

"Yes," Lizzie said. "I saw him. Minka, listen, he was—" But at that moment Father came in, grabbing a kitchen towel and mopping his face and hair. Minka put a finger to her lips.

"Tell me later. When we're alone."

When Father took the towel away, he did a double take. "What's happened here? Minka's up at last!"

"I'm better, Father," Minka said.

"So you are," he cried. "I'm very glad to see it!" He wasn't much given to hugs, but he pulled Minka close and stroked her head.

Lizzie climbed to the loft to change her soaked clothes. She jumped every time thunder sounded.

The boys came back in dripping. Stefan looked half drowned, his hair plastered to his head, his shirt a little waterfall, his boots squelching on the wooden floor.

"Take off those wet clothes, child. You'll catch your death!" Mother scolded. She helped Stefan pull off his soaked clothing and boots, wrapped him in a blanket, and hung his shirt and pants over a chair by the stove. Jakob shook his head when Mother tried to insist he do the same. He simply took a towel and rubbed his hair till it stood on end.

"We put Kosmy in the stable and gave him some hay," Stefan reported.

"Good boy!" Father told him, and Stefan glowed

from the compliment. Mother passed around tea and cocoa, then began to make supper, and the children sat on the sofa—Jakob on the floor, because he was so wet—and drank. But when Lizzie reached for her cup, Minka noticed the damp kerchief wrapped around her hand.

"What happened here? Give me your hand!" she demanded. She untied Mistress Klara's kerchief and drew in a deep breath when she saw Lizzie's wound.

"A—a branch—in the storm," Lizzie stammered. Not quite a lie. She would tell Minka later, when there was no chance of Mother hearing. Mother would never believe it.

"Do you have any honey?" Jakob asked. "It keeps a cut from getting infected."

Minka went to the kitchen and returned with a jar of honey and a cloth. Gently Jakob held Lizzie's hand steady and dabbed honey on the cut. Then he wound a fresh cloth around it and tied it securely.

"It shouldn't leave a scar," he said, satisfied.

"You could be a doctor, Jakob!" Minka said.

"I'm hoping that someday I will," he told her.

"Really? I thought you were going to farm!"

"That's what my pa thinks—but I've been read-ing about medicine, even spending some time with

Dr. Śmigly for a while now. I hate farming, and I hate the farm. When I think of spending my whole life ploughing and hoeing . . . well, I just don't want to."

Minka nodded. It was clear she understood Jakob's feelings.

"But medicine—it's amazing. To learn about sicknesses, about healing, about what treatments and herbs can help—I love it."

"He dosed me when I was throwing up from eating too many walnuts," Stefan said. "It worked really well. But now I can't eat walnuts anymore because I feel like throwing up when I just look at them."

"And what about when your pa finds out?" Minka asked, tousling Stefan's wet hair.

Jakob looked down. "He found one of my books. But he thinks I'm reading it just to be more useful around the farm. In case one of us has an accident, or falls sick."

Minka nodded again. She knew Jakob's father.

"Pa will smack him silly when he finds out," Stefan said frankly, and Jakob scowled at him.

"Be quiet, Stef!" he commanded. "Now, how does the hand feel, Lizzie?"

"Better," Lizzie said. "It's not a sharp pain anymore. More of a dull ache."

"Good. We'd best get back," Jakob said. "It sounds like the rain has slacked off. Stef, you're going to have to get back into those wet clothes."

"Yuck," Stefan said cheerfully, shucking off the blanket and pulling on his soaked trousers. "Oh, they're cold!"

"We'll walk fast," Jakob assured him. "You can get dry at home."

"If Pa doesn't make us go right out into the fields," Stefan said. "He's going to be so mad that we were gone all day!"

"Tell him how you helped me at the market," Lizzie urged. "He can't blame you for that."

Jakob shrugged. "He'll do what he wants."

Mother couldn't convince them to stay and eat, try as she might. The boys waved as they walked down the muddy lane. The rain had become no more than a light mist rising from the damp ground.

That night, Minka climbed the ladder to the loft for the first time in weeks. But Lizzie found she didn't want to talk about Emil, even though they were alone. She wanted to make sense of him in her own mind first. So she turned her face to the wall and feigned sleep, and though Minka tried to rouse her, she refused to talk.

Lizzie slept that night as she hadn't in weeks. She only woke when a slant of sunlight fell across her face.

"Minka!" she cried, peering over the edge of the loft and seeing that Minka had opened the front door, a basket in her hand. Lizzie scrambled down the ladder. "Oh, it wasn't a dream. You're really awake!"

"I'm awake," Minka agreed, placing the basket on the kitchen table. "And so are you. How does your hand feel?"

Lizzie looked down at her bandaged hand. She wiggled her fingers. "It doesn't hurt a bit!"

"That's wonderful!" Minka said. "Jakob did a good job."

"He's a good person," Lizzie said. "He was so brave at the market...with Emil." She was ready to talk about it, now that she felt rested.

"How did Emil look?" Minka asked. She tried to sound casual, but Lizzie could see from the gray that mixed with her voice's rose colors that she was unsettled. "Did he say he missed me? Was he worried about me?"

"No, Minka," Lizzie said bluntly. "He was horrible. I don't like him."

"You don't understand," Minka insisted. "You will someday."

"Tell me now," Lizzie said. "I want to understand it. Really, I do."

Minka gave her a sidelong look. "You have to promise not to say anything mean."

"I promise."

"It's just..." Minka thought for a moment. "When he looks at me, I feel alive. I feel beautiful. I feel like...like a piece of his fruit. Ripe to bursting. He makes me want...everything. Oh, never mind. I'm doing a bad job of it!"

Lizzie chewed on her lip. "No, you're not. I can understand that he makes you feel beautiful. You *are* beautiful. Jakob said so. But how can you feel like fruit? You're a person."

Minka smiled. "Haven't you ever felt like something other than a person? Don't you feel free, like a bird, when school lets out for the summer?"

"Do you mean like I could fly? But people can't fly." This was getting more and more confusing.

"It's a metaphor," Minka said. "Like we learned in school, remember? A comparison."

"Metaphors are so stupid!" Lizzie protested. "I

never understood why Mistress Lena would compare people to foxes, or mice. Or being sick to being like a dog. Dogs are almost never sick!"

"Oh, Lizzie!" Minka laughed. "You are so...*you*."

"Who else would I be?" Lizzie asked, bewildered. The conversation had gotten completely out of hand. "But here's the other thing. Emil said you would rise and come to him. And I think maybe...when he said it...that's when you woke up."

"Oh, that's lovely," Minka sighed. "It's as if I could sense that he wanted me to wake, isn't it?"

That wasn't what Lizzie had meant at all. It was supposed to sound eerie, *sinister*—not romantic. But nothing she told Minka about Emil seemed to change the way she felt about him. She had a terrible feeling that Minka would have to change her own mind.

But she tried again. She had to. "Jakob couldn't see or hear him, Minka."

Minka furrowed her brow. "What do you mean?"

"Just what I said. He couldn't see or hear Emil."

"But that's..." Minka's voice trailed off.

"Impossible?" Lizzie suggested. "I know. It is. And yet it happened. But Jakob could *feel* Emil, when he hit him."

"What? Jakob hit Emil? Why?"

"No. Emil hit Jakob."

"Emil would *never* do such a thing!" Minka cried.

"Oh, but he did," Lizzie assured her. "So hard that Jakob flew in the air. Didn't you wonder about that bruise on his cheek?"

"I thought–I thought it must have been his father."

"Not this time," Lizzie said. "And the cut on my hand–that was him, too. At least I think it was."

"You said it was a tree branch!"

"He made the tree branch scratch me. He raised his hand and the limb came down and hurt me." Lizzie could hear how farfetched it was, even as she said it. But it was the truth. "Minka, Emil is...he's *wrong*. He's a bad person. I'm not–I'm not even sure he *is* a person."

Minka stared at her. It sounded ridiculous, even to Lizzie, but she had to keep going. "Have you ever heard of a zdusze?"

Minka frowned. "You mean from the old tales? Yes. We had a book with a story about a zdusze when we were little. Remember? It was a scary story, and you hated it. You made Mother hide the book away."

Lizzie had forgotten, but now she remembered it as clear as anything. After Mother had read them the story, about a forest goblin that stole children, she'd had nightmares for days. She'd gone around pinching Minka to make sure she wasn't just wearing a human disguise, like the zduszes. The goblins in the story had looked like people, except to children. Children could see the shapes of their real selves. Perhaps like the strange, single glimpse Lizzie'd had of Emil at the market—a glimpse of something not quite human shrouded just below the surface.

"You're not saying that Emil is one of *those,* are you?" Minka asked. "Because that would just be daft."

"I know," Lizzie said. "It sounds daft. But I think it's true."

Minka scowled. "Stop it, Lizzie," she said harshly. "It's not like you to make up stories. Why would you do that?" Then her face softened. "You know, there's nothing to be afraid of—we'll always be sisters. Close as close can be. You don't need to worry that Emil will take that away from us. Lizzie and Minka, just we two—it will always be like in our song. Come on, sing it with me. *Lizzie and Minka, me and you. Lizzie and Minka, just we two—*"

"He made you sick, Minka!" Lizzie burst out. "It was him—his fruit. He nearly killed you!"

"That's enough!" Minka's fingers curled into fists,

and she stamped her foot hard on the floor. She turned away without speaking, grabbed her basket, and went out through the open door to the garden.

When she was gone, Lizzie went to look for the book. Eventually she found it, pushed to the back of the little bookcase in Mother and Father's room. It told the story of twins, a boy and a girl, who were lured into a forest by a goblin only they could see. There were illustrations of the boy and girl, of their house, of the dark forest, but no pictures of the goblin, only descriptions. It had red eyes, sharp claws, even sharper teeth.

There was a part of the tale she'd forgotten, though. When the twins disappeared, their parents went for help to someone called a prorok—a woman who was a sort of fortune-teller. An illustration showed her wearing a colorful shawl and ruffled skirt, sitting in a darkened room. For a minute Lizzie thought she might have remembered the story wrong. Maybe the prorok saved the twins…? But no. All the prorok could do was tell the grieving parents that their children were gone for good.

Lizzie shuddered and shoved the book back into the bookcase.

She went to the door to check on Minka. She still could hardly believe her sister was up and around, looking so well and rested.

Minka wasn't in the garden, though. She was sitting beneath the cherry tree, leaning against it. Her head was tipped back, pressed against its bark; Lizzie could see the smooth creamy line of her throat. And she could see the blush-pink puffs of her words. Minka was whispering—whispering to the tree.

CHAPTER 9

Jakob came back the next morning. He wasn't really needed, since Minka was awake and Lizzie could leave her to work with Father, but Lizzie was beginning to think that Jakob's reasons for visiting went beyond his desire to help out. Minka was mixing dough for pierogies, so she just gave Jakob a floury wave. Lizzie pulled him aside as soon as he walked in the door.

"There's more strangeness," she hissed.

His eyebrows went up. "What's happened?"

"Minka is...talking to the cherry tree. The one that grew from the fruit Emil gave her."

"Talking to it? It's a *tree*."

"Well, I know that," Lizzie said, exasperated. "But she's whispering to it. She was out there last evening, and again this morning. And I...well, I think it might be whispering back."

Jakob opened his mouth, then closed it again.

"Are you talking about me?" Minka called from the kitchen.

"No," said Jakob, and "Yes," said Lizzie.

Minka laughed. "Well, stop it!"

"Jakob," Lizzie said, low, "have you ever heard of a prorok?"

"A prorok? Yes. In fact, I know one, or she calls herself one," Jakob said. "She's my...second cousin? Third? Second once removed? I'm not sure. On my mother's side. She lives in Elza. She comes by every now and then to be sure Pa is feeding us enough. I've heard she reads fortunes in her house, or something like that."

"Will you go with me to visit her?"

"I haven't been to her house in years. And you— you want to go into town? Why?"

Lizzie told Jakob about the story in the book she'd read. He looked doubtful about the idea. "If that prorok wasn't able to help, why do you think Cousin Jadwiga could?"

"I don't know what else to do!" Lizzie cried, and Minka turned from her bowl of dough.

"Stop it, Lizzie," she said sternly. "You don't have to worry about me. I'm awake, and I'm fine!"

"He said you would wake up," Lizzie said, her

voice very low. "He said it, that boy—or whatever he was. He's not right, Minka. He's bad."

Minka drew back her lips in a snarl, and Lizzie recoiled. She'd never, ever seen such an expression on her sister's face before.

"Be quiet," Minka hissed. "I know what you're doing. You're jealous, is all. You don't want me to be in love. You don't want me to go away with Emil. You want me to stay here and grow old taking care of you until I rot and *die*. Well, you can't make me stay, Lizzie! *I won't!*"

Lizzie couldn't speak. Jakob looked shocked, but he stayed silent.

It was hard to believe that such dreadful words had come from Minka's mouth. And none of it was true. Was it?

Mother came in from the garden then, and Minka turned back to her cooking as if she had never spoken.

While the onions sizzled, Lizzie asked permission to go to town with Jakob. "Father doesn't need us today," she said. "He's mostly just sharpening tools and getting ready for harvest."

"And you want to go?" Mother was taken aback.

"I know an herbalist in town," Jakob said. "A

cousin of mine. She can give us some concoctions to make sure Minka stays well."

"In that case...yes, Lizzie, you can go. It will be good for you, meeting new people. Be back by supper."

Minka snorted and slammed her mixing bowl into the sink with a good deal more force than was necessary. "Gently, Minka!" Mother admonished her. "I know you're feeling lively, but there's no need to break the crockery!" Lizzie and Jacob hurried out.

On the walk into town, Lizzie couldn't get Minka's unkind words out of her mind. If she was honest—and she always was—she had to admit some of them were true. She *didn't* want her sister to leave. She *did* want Minka to stay and watch over her. She'd never pictured any other future than living in her own house, working Father's land, sleeping next to Minka in their cozy loft—or at the most, having her live nearby, married to a local boy, maybe teaching in their school. Sometimes she imagined being auntie to Minka's children, and that was a lovely thought.

But it was clearly not the story that Minka wanted her life to tell. It was terrible to Lizzie to try to think of a future without her sister—but it was what Minka longed for. Lizzie hadn't known it. Maybe Emil was right. Maybe she didn't know Minka at all.

⚜

The air was hot and still, and Lizzie was sweaty by the time they reached the town gate. Jakob led her down one cobbled alley and up another. They stopped in front of a tall, charcoal-colored door in a tall, narrow house. In its center was a door knocker unlike any Lizzie had ever seen. It was a brass arm, as lifelike as brass could be. Even the wrinkles on the knuckles looked real. It held a sphere, and when Lizzie looked closely it seemed as if she could see figures and faces in that sphere, shifting and turning. She blinked hard, and the shapes were gone. Jakob lifted the knocker and let it fall against the painted wooden door: the sphere struck a brass-lined indentation with a multicolored, undulating *thump*.

There was a long wait. Lizzie grew more and more anxious. But at last the door swung open with a creak. A voice from within, sienna-colored, said, "Do come in."

Jakob led the way inside. A woman stood just behind the door. The light was murky, but Lizzie could see that she was dressed much like the prorok in her book's illustration. She wore a woven shawl, even in the heat, and her skirt was patchwork with a ruffle at the bottom. Her hair was braided in a hundred braids from scalp to ends and tied at the nape of her neck. Though her face was unlined, there was something ageless about her. She could have been thirty or seventy.

"Cousin Jadwiga!" Jakob said. He and the prorok exchanged a rather formal kiss. "I hope you don't mind us dropping in."

"Not in the least, Cousin Jakob," the prorok said. "You have grown up a bit in the last five years!"

"I hope so," Jakob said, and the prorok laughed.

"Come, sit down. Have some tea. Tell me why you are here. I suspect it is not just a neighborly visit."

"It's not," Jakob said.

The prorok led the way down the dim hallway, and Lizzie followed Jakob, her head swiveling to take in the oddness of the house. The ceilings in the rooms they passed were immensely high; Lizzie couldn't even see them when she looked upward. The hall itself was lined with gilt-framed pictures that she would have loved to stop and study, but they moved past them too quickly for her to make out more than a few shadowy shapes.

They stopped in what Lizzie assumed was a parlor, as dark and high-ceilinged as the rest of the house. There were windows, but they were draped in maroon velvet that swept to the floor. The prorok motioned to them to sit. Lizzie found her way to an armchair; when she lowered herself to its cushion, it gave off a puff of dust that made her sneeze.

"I'll have tea in just a minute," the prorok said, and disappeared through a swinging door.

Lizzie sat very upright on her chair, her hands clasped nervously in front of her.

"What do you think?" Jakob asked.

"This is a very curious house," Lizzie said uneasily.

"Isn't it?" Jakob agreed. "Cousin Jadwiga likes atmosphere. Apparently people are willing to pay more if they get a certain kind of atmosphere."

Lizzie nodded. "Does she charge a lot?" She tried to remember if she had any coppers in her pocket.

"Not for us," Jakob assured her. "I'm family."

In a few minutes the prorok was back, carrying a tray with a very tarnished silver tea service balanced on it. She poured and handed Jakob a cup, then passed one to Lizzie. Lizzie took a sip. It tasted like mud.

"Lemon?" the prorok asked brightly.

"Yes, please," Lizzie said, and Jakob added, "Do you have any sugar?" They both sugared their tea liberally and squeezed lemon into their cups. With the additions, it was almost drinkable.

"Now," the prorok said, sitting and ignoring the dust she raised, "who is this charming girl, and what can I do for you both?"

Lizzie was silent, so Jakob introduced her quickly, and then described Minka's situation—her meeting with Emil; the fruit; her hair loss; her long sleep. Her sudden, strange awakening.

The prorok steepled her hands together and hummed after she heard the story. Finally she spoke. "There have been three others that I have heard of," she said.

"Three?" Lizzie repeated, horrified. "I've only heard about Janina."

"Yes, Janina," the prorok agreed. "But two more. One from farther north, and one from Elza. That was several years ago now—ten? Twenty? I lose track of time."

"What happened to the other girls?"

"Hmm." The prorok thought for a moment. "The one from up north, I don't believe I ever heard."

"And the one from Elza?"

"Oh, she died," the prorok said. She didn't seem to notice Lizzie's sharp inhale. "Nobody knew what was wrong with her. Her parents thought it was a summer fever. The doctor—it was old Dr. Kluk, do you remember him, cousin?"

Jakob nodded. "He retired years ago, didn't he?"

"That's right. He was completely at a loss. He treated the poor girl with herbs and cupping, but of course nothing helped. When I heard all the details, I was quite sure that her illness was caused by a zdusze."

Lizzie let out a long breath. "That's what we've been thinking," she said. "But why? What would a zdusze want from Minka?"

The prorok sighed. "The legends say they seize little children to siphon off their energy, their vigor. But why girls, girls of Minka's age? To take as wives, I imagine."

"To take as wives," Lizzie echoed, shuddering. "He said he loves Minka. And I think she would marry him if she could."

"All of the cases followed the same pattern," the prorok said. "A girl at market. A boy with fruit. A girl who gives the boy something of value. A girl graying

and weakening, failing and sleeping. A girl disap-
pearing, or dying."

Lizzie was quiet for a moment.

"What object of value did Minka give the boy,
dear?" the prorok asked gently.

"She gave him a lock of her hair."

"Ah," the prorok said. "She has made a pledge,
then. That is not good."

"But what can we do?" Lizzie cried. "Will he take
her away? Will he kill her? How can we save her?"

"You must try to fight him with his own weapon,"
the prorok replied. "Yours is real, his is not."

Lizzie turned questioning eyes to Jakob. "What
weapon? Fruit? Magic? I don't have those things!"

The prorok was silent.

"Cousin Jadwiga? What do you mean by 'his own
weapon'?" Jakob asked. But the prorok didn't answer.
She seemed to be in a kind of trance, her eyes closed,
her fingers still together in a steeple shape. She
swayed gently back and forth on the sofa.

Jakob shook his head. "She gets like this, I've
heard. I don't think there's anything we can do."

Lizzie was frantic. "But she hasn't helped at all!
We have to do something!"

"She won't wake for hours, maybe days," Jakob said. "We may as well go. Wait here until I get the herbs I need for Minka from the kitchen."

"But–but–" Lizzie sputtered. Jakob rose from the sofa and placed his teacup on the tray. Helpless, Lizzie did the same. She waited until Jakob came back, two small packets in hand; then she followed him out of the room, looking back to see the prorok rocking gently on the sofa, humming her reddish-brown hum to herself.

Outside again, Lizzie blinked in the bright sunshine, nearly blinded after the dimness of the prorok's house. She clenched her fists in frustration. "Now what?" she demanded. "That was useless!"

Jakob shrugged helplessly. "I don't know, Lizzie. Maybe if we spoke to the parents of the girl... it's our only lead."

"You mean the one from Elza? But who is she? And how could that help?"

"It might not help. But what choice do we have? I can find out her name from old Dr. Kluk. I'm pretty sure he's still alive."

More people to meet, to talk to. Lizzie could hardly bear the thought. She wanted to be home, wanted it so badly she could almost see her cottage, smell Minka's pierogies browning in butter. But she nodded glumly. "All right. Let's see him."

"We'll ask at the apothecary's," Jakob said. "I'm sure they'll know where the doctor lives."

Jakob let Lizzie wait outside while he ducked into the apothecary's shop. A moment later he was out again. "It's this way," he said, leading Lizzie down the street.

Dr. Kluk's home wasn't far from the prorok's. It was a small, ramshackle house set back a bit from the cobblestone alley. Its front yard was a tangle of weeds. When Jakob knocked on the front door, it was quickly opened by a small woman with a blue kerchief tied over her hair.

"What do you want?" she demanded. Her voice was a puff of mustard yellow.

"Is Dr. Kluk in?" Jakob asked politely.

"And where else would he be but in?" the woman said. "Who's asking?"

"I'm Jakob Nowak, and this is Lizzie. We would like to speak with him. It's a—a health matter."

"Hmph," the woman snorted, but she backed into the house and allowed Lizzie and Jakob to come in.

The entryway was barely passable. Towers of

papers and books were stacked everywhere, all of them taller than Lizzie, with only a small path left to walk through. Lizzie held her arms tight to her sides as she moved down the hall, but she brushed against one pile, and it wobbled and then crashed down, knocking a second pile over.

"Now see what you've done!" the woman cried.

"Sorry," Lizzie said. "I didn't mean to."

"Clumsy oaf," the woman muttered, but she continued on.

They stopped at a closed door off the hallway, and the woman knocked sharply and then entered. "Doctor!" she shouted. "You have visitors!"

"He must be hard of hearing," Jakob whispered to Lizzie.

They walked into the room behind the woman. This room, too, was a jumble of papers and books: on the floor, on a desk, even on the side tables that flanked the bed in which a small figure reclined. Dr. Kluk was a tiny, white-haired man, his face a map of wrinkles, his eyes clouded and unseeing. The quilt on his bed was pulled up to his neck, though the room was stifling hot.

"Good afternoon, Dr. Kluk!" Jakob said in a loud voice.

"You don't need to shout," Dr. Kluk said in a high, fluty voice. "Don't mind Mistress Iwa. She likes yelling. My hearing is fine, just fine."

"I see," Jakob said in a lower voice. "We're here to ask you about a patient from several years ago. A girl."

"Eh?" Dr. Kluk said. "I didn't say to whisper."

"A girl! A young woman!" Jakob repeated, louder. "An old patient!"

"Well, is she young or old? Make up your mind!" Dr. Kluk said.

Jakob gritted his teeth in frustration. "She was young. This happened some years ago. She became ill after eating fruit. Her hair turned gray. She died."

"Did you say she died?"

"Yes!" Jakob shouted. Lizzie could tell he was becoming exasperated.

"Shh, shh," Dr. Kluk scolded. "Now let me think. A girl...fruit...hair...it must be in my notes. Perhaps we can find it."

Lizzie looked at the piles of papers. Find a note from ten or twenty years ago in all that? It would take days. Weeks!

"Perhaps you could just try to remember," she suggested.

"Nothing wrong with my memory!" Dr. Kluk snapped. "Of course I can remember. Let's see. Fruit…hair…" He began mumbling to himself.

Lizzie shook her head. "Jacob, perhaps we should go," she murmured.

"Go! Why would you go? I thought you wanted information!" Dr. Kluk cried.

How had he heard her? Was he deaf or not? Despite the seriousness of their visit, Lizzie felt a laugh rising. She pushed it down. "Sorry," she said. "Do you remember the girl?"

"Eh?"

"Do you remember the girl?" Lizzie shouted.

"No need to shout!" Dr. Kluk said. "Nothing wrong with my hearing! Of course I remember her. Ada, her name was. Ada Babis. A pretty girl, charming. Such a shame. She had a fever. I remember her well. Nothing wrong with my memory!"

"Ada Babis," Lizzie repeated. "Do you recall where she lived?"

"Eh?"

"Where she lived! Do you remember?"

"You are a very noisy child," Dr. Kluk said reprovingly. "Of course I remember where she lived. Bukowa Lane, near the town wall. Number fifty-two."

"You do have a good memory!" Lizzie said.

"Eh?"

A giggle escaped Lizzie. Dr. Kluk squinted at her. "Are you laughing at me, young lady?"

"I—well, yes," Lizzie admitted.

There was a silence, and then Dr. Kluk let out a high-pitched cackle. "Always glad to entertain!" he said. "Nothing wrong with my sense of humor!"

"No indeed," Lizzie said. Her voice wavered with repressed laughter. "Thank you, Doctor. We'll let you rest now."

"Eh?"

"We'll let you rest!" Lizzie repeated.

"No need to shout!" Dr. Kluk shouted. "And I have no need to rest. All I do is rest! Stay for tea!"

"We can't," Jakob said. "But I'll come back if you'd like, and we can discuss medicine."

"Discuss meddling?" Dr. Kluk said. "Take that up with Mistress Iwa. All she does is meddle. See what a mess she's made of my notes!"

Mistress Iwa, standing in the doorway, let out a loud sniff. "It's all just as he wants it," she said.

"I heard that!" Dr. Kluk cried. "Nothing wrong with my hearing!"

"Goodbye, Dr. Kluk!" Jakob shouted. "Thank you for your help!"

"Goodbye!" Lizzie echoed.

"Come back soon," Dr. Kluk said. "You're very loud, both of you, but I like visitors!"

Lizzie and Jakob promised they would, and meant it. Then, carefully, they made their way to the front door, knocking over another couple of stacks of papers and books on the way. Mistress Iwa held the door open for them and fixed them with a glare.

"He won't sleep a bit tonight," she complained. "You've completely overexcited him."

"So sorry," Lizzie said. As the door slammed behind them, she and Jakob both burst into laughter.

"Oh, oh, oh," Jakob said, holding his sides.

"Nothing wrong with his housekeeper!" Lizzie gasped.

It was several minutes before they were calm enough to speak. "Can we find the Babises?" Jakob finally managed.

"Number fifty-two Bukowa Lane," Lizzie said.

"Nothing wrong with your memory!" Jakob said, and Lizzie giggled again. "We'll talk to them. Then we'll head home."

"All right," Lizzie said. Her worries came marching back. Now came the hard part: talking to grieving parents.

Parents whose daughter had died after eating fruit from a zdusze.

CHAPTER 10

Lizzie and Jakob walked along the quiet street, counting off the house numbers. Number 12, 23, 37, 45. There it was: number 52.

It was a pretty whitewashed house, its walls painted with flowers and vines like Lizzie's home. In front was a big yard filled with late-summer flowers. The chimney had a storks' nest, and an enormous bird sat on it, watching them with sharp, beady eyes. Lizzie focused on the stork as she walked up to the front door. She loved storks—their beautiful fringed wings and long orange beaks, their ungainly bodies so graceful in flight. She imagined that the stork was bringing her luck, as they were said to do for those who lived in houses where they chose to build their nests. Maybe the Babises would have the answers she needed.

That idea gave Lizzie the strength to knock on the door, and it was opened by a little girl. She couldn't have been more than five or six years old. Her reddish-brown hair was braided in two plaits so tight that her eyebrows were pulled high on her forehead, giving her a surprised look, and her grin showed two missing front teeth.

"Hello!" she said, her voice a cheery bright green.

"Hello," Lizzie replied. "Um...is this the Babises' house?"

"I'm Marta. Who are you?"

"I'm Lizzie. This is Jakob. We—"

A woman came up behind the girl, wiping her hands on her apron. She put a hand on Marta's shoulder. "Can I help you?"

With an effort, Lizzie met the woman's eyes. They seemed kind. "I–I hope so. We're looking for information. About a girl? She...she was sick?" Lizzie didn't want to go into any detail in front of the child.

The woman drew in a sharp breath and stepped back. "I see. All right. Come in." She turned and began walking into the house, and Lizzie quickly followed, Jakob shutting the door behind them with a click. Marta ran ahead into the kitchen, where a pot simmered on the stove.

"Marta, go play in the yard," her mother instructed.

Marta turned her mouth down in a pout. "I want to talk to the people!" she protested.

"Maybe later," the woman said. She bent to give the girl a kiss on the top of her head, and Marta shrugged and dashed out the kitchen door, where Lizzie could see her do an awkward cartwheel on the grass as a small spotted dog nipped at her ankles.

"Sit," the woman invited. "Tell me what you want." They sat at the wooden table, its top covered with an embroidered cloth.

"It's my sister, Minka," Lizzie said. "She went to the market, met a boy. He gave her some fruit. Now she's sick."

Mistress Babis gasped. "Yes," she whispered. "Like Ada."

"Your daughter."

The woman nodded. "I was young when she was born. She was our only child. Such a smart girl, so pretty and sweet. And her embroidery—it was like art. Here, this is one of the pillows she did." She stood and went to the sofa, picked up a pillow, and brought it to Lizzie. The embroidery really was remarkable: a flowering tree graced the center, orange and pink and yellow, and on either side were embroidered roosters with multicolored tail feathers.

"It's beautiful," Lizzie said. She handed the pillow back.

"It was nearly ten years ago now that it happened. A terrible time, terrible. No one knew what ailed her—what killed her. The doctor couldn't help. Nobody could help." Tears trembled on Mistress Babis's lashes.

Lizzie felt guilty for bringing painful memories back to this nice woman. "I'm so sorry," she murmured. "If you don't want to talk about it ..."

"Oh, my dear, she is never far from my thoughts," Mistress Babis said. "It's all right."

"She met a boy ...? Like Minka did?"

"At the market," Mistress Babis said. "He sold fruit. She fell in love, or so she told me before she died."

"And you think he was ..."

"A zdusze. A goblin. I'm sure of it."

"Why do you think so?" Lizzie asked.

"I believe in those old stories," Mistress Babis said. "I always have. The zduszes entice our children with what they want most. For the little ones, it can be a sweet, or a playmate. For the older girls, it's love. Always love. The fruit is just a lure."

Jakob drew in a deep breath, and Lizzie nodded slowly.

"I've always felt it was my fault," Mistress Babis went on. A tear dropped on the tablecloth with a golden *plink*. "I think Ada didn't know how much she was loved, here in her family. How much she was valued. We didn't hug or say those words. I assumed she knew, but how can a child know such a thing if she isn't told? So when the boy came and promised her everything, she was his completely. He wanted her to come to him—to meet him in Noc Forest—but we restrained her. And then she was too weak to go…"

She clasped her hands on the tabletop, lost in her thoughts. Then she seemed to remember where she was and blinked.

"I'm sorry, child," she said to Lizzie. "Maybe you are too young to be hearing these things."

"No," Lizzie replied, "I had to hear them. I had to know, so I can help my sister."

"Of course," Mistress Babis said. "I can see that you love your sister very much."

"More than anything."

"And you?" Mistress Babis turned to Jakob. He

flushed and looked down. "Poor lad," she said, shaking her head.

The kitchen door crashed open, and Marta ran in. "Can I come in yet? Can I talk to the people?" she cried. The dog came in after her and jumped up on Lizzie, its stubby tail wagging. Dogs made Lizzie nervous; she only knew cats and donkeys. But this one was cute and small, so she gave it a timid pat. Its whole body wriggled with pleasure.

"Do you want some cake?" Marta asked Lizzie. "Because I do want some cake, and if you say you want some, then Mama will give me some, too."

Lizzie looked at Mistress Babis and saw her mouth twitch, so she smiled and said, "I would love some cake, thank you very much!"

Over cream-filled karpatka cake, Mistress Babis told Lizzie and Jakob how, three years after Ada's death, storks came and built a nest in their chimney.

"My husband actually built us a new chimney, so we could let them have the old one. We wanted them to stay." She smiled, remembering. "I had trouble believing we could ever have good luck again, but it was only a year later that this little one was born."

Marta grinned, her face smeared with cake

custard. "I'm the good luck," she said. It was clear she knew this part of the story well.

"I was old to have a child, but here she is. My good-luck baby." Mistress Babis ruffled her daughter's hair.

"You are quite an old mama, but I love you just the same," Marta said cheerfully.

Lizzie watched them carefully. She could see that Mistress Babis was determined not to make the same mistake with Marta that she had with Ada. Marta was a child who basked in her mother's love.

When they had finished their cake, Lizzie and Jakob thanked Mistress Babis. Lizzie let Marta give her a quick hug that left a splotch of custard on her skirt.

They started home as the sun sank low in the sky. "That wasn't very helpful," Jakob said with a sigh.

"No," Lizzie admitted. "Though what Mistress Babis said about love was—well, interesting." She tried to think if she ever told Minka she loved her, plainly, in just those words. She thought not. She didn't say such things to anyone. Neither did Mother or Father. But wouldn't Minka know anyway?

Lizzie took the packets of the prorok's herbs from

Jakob as they parted. Once she reached her home, she put them in the kitchen cupboard, then went to join Mother weeding the garden. They worked on separate rows, and somehow, Lizzie found herself alone with the cherry tree.

She stopped and stared at its ghastly face. "What are you?" she whispered. "Why does Minka talk to you?"

A sigh of wind rustled the leaves.

Lizzie looked around. None of the other trees or bushes moved. But the cherry tree's rustling grew louder. It seemed almost to form words.

"*Shhhhhhhhhheeeee lovesssssssss meeeeeeeee. Shhhhhhhhhheeee lovesssssss meeeeeeeee.*"

Lizzie backed away, her hands over her mouth. The sounds became clearer.

"*Shheee lovesss meee. Mmmore than she loves you. She loves me. She has come to me. She is with me.*"

By the last words, the tree was speaking in Emil's voice.

Lizzie spun and ran. "Minka!" she screamed. "Minka, where are you? Minka!"

Mother looked up from her weeding. "Lizzie! She's in the house. No need to shout!"

146

Lizzie dashed back into the cottage and raced up the ladder to the loft. No one was there. Panicked, she felt under Minka's pillow, where her sister had placed the locket Emil gave her.

It was gone.

CHAPTER 11

Lizzie sat in the loft, gasping for breath, trying to figure out what to do. Minka's beloved locket was gone; Minka was gone. She was with Emil. Lizzie was certain of it.

She had to get Jakob. No one else knew the whole story. No one else would understand. She scrambled back down the ladder, out the door, and down the lane. Behind her she heard Mother call, "Lizzie! Where are you going?" but she sprinted onward.

When she reached Jakob's father's fields, she was breathless and sweaty. In the distance she could see Jakob and Stefan hoeing the beets. She waved her arms wildly, and after a moment Stefan noticed. He poked his brother, and both boys started toward her.

"What's wrong?" Jakob called. "Is it Minka? Is she sick again?"

"She's—she's *gone*!" Lizzie shouted.

They reached her side, and Jakob said, "What do you mean, gone?"

Lizzie bent over to catch her breath. "Gone. Packed up. She's left. She's gone to Emil. In Noc Forest, I think."

"The goblin?" Stefan said, his eyes wide. "Why did she go with him?"

Lizzie shook her head. "I don't know. I don't know."

Jakob put a hand on her shoulder. She didn't shrug it off. "She'll be all right, Lizzie. We'll find her."

"Where are we going to look?" Stefan asked. "What will we tell Pa?"

Jakob and Lizzie exchanged a glance. They couldn't take Stefan, Lizzie knew. He'd get in the way, cause trouble, put himself and them in danger. They just couldn't.

"We'll tell him we had to go help Lizzie's pa," Jakob said firmly. "Nothing about goblins, you hear? You run to the barn and get the jug of water and the sausages we left in there. We're going to need food and water."

"I can do that," Stefan said. "I'll be fast. I'll be right back!" He spun around and sprinted in the direction of the barn.

"Come on," Jakob said to Lizzie. "If we're out of sight when he gets back, he might not follow us. It's getting late, and he doesn't like the dark."

They raced down the lane and ducked into the Wood so they wouldn't have to go past Lizzie's cottage, where her mother would see them and stop them. Lizzie wasn't sure how she felt about lying to Stefan, fooling him like that. She knew he'd be terribly upset when he realized they'd gone without him. But they had to. And she didn't have time to worry about his feelings now.

"You said Noc Forest?" Jakob asked as they ran.

"That's the only place I could think of!" Lizzie replied. "It's what Mistress Babis said—that the goblin wanted to meet her daughter there, remember? I don't know where else to try!"

"It's as good a guess as any," Jakob said.

Noc Forest was a quarter of a mile past Elza's northern gate. They sped down the road to town, passed through the main gate, cut across the market square, and dashed out the northern gate, saying nothing to the city guards or anyone else they passed.

They reached the edge of the forest as dusk began to settle in, and, for the first time, hesitated.

Peering into the shadowy depths, Lizzie shivered. It was nothing like her own Wood. She had never entered Noc Forest; people got lost there all the time. There were tales about bandits, about children eaten by wolves. Mother said they weren't true, but it was easy to believe. The few paths were winding and twisted, and the trees pressed together, blocking what little light came from the setting sun. A moment after they'd stepped off the lane, they were in darkness.

"How do we know which path to take?" Jakob asked.

"I don't know," Lizzie said. "We can come back and start again if we have to."

But she knew that wasn't true. She knew they didn't have much time. She had to choose the right path. So at each branching, she closed her eyes and thought of Minka, and then she headed in the direction that felt right.

The silence was nearly complete, save for the gray-blue crunch of leaves underfoot and Lizzie's own thrumming lilac heartbeat. The air grew damper. They passed stands of birches covered with moss so intensely green that even in the dimness it glistened. The ground too was mossy, and it sank beneath their feet so they felt as if they were walking on sponges. From the rotting logs that lay scattered near the path came an eerie blue-green glow.

"What is that?" Lizzie said, low. "Is it goblin magic?"

"I don't think so," Jakob said. "It's fox fire. I don't know what causes it, but I've seen it on wet wood before."

"It's eerie."

"It is," Jakob agreed. "But at least it makes it a little easier to see."

The path narrowed, and Jakob followed behind, so Lizzie didn't notice when he disappeared. But she heard the splash—saw the lavender color of it—and a moment later came Jakob's terrified shout.

"Help! Lizzie, help!"

Lizzie spun around. In the dim light she saw a hand sticking up through the moss, waving wildly. For a moment she thought Jakob had fallen into a pit, a hole in the ground, but as she took the next step she realized her boot was submerged in water. The moss was *floating*, floating on a bog, and Jakob had plunged through it.

She pulled her foot back and threw herself to firmer ground, feeling the wetness of the moss soak through her clothes. She grabbed the waving hand

and pulled with all her strength. Hand, arm, shoulder came out of the water. Then Jakob's face, as he choked and spat water.

"Something—" he gasped, "something is dragging me down! Pull harder, Lizzie!"

But she wasn't strong enough to pull Jakob up.

"Keep your head up!" she shouted. "Wait! I have to get a branch!"

Moving as fast as she dared on the boggy ground, she scrabbled about until she found a fallen branch that looked thick and strong enough to hold Jakob's weight. But she when got back to where she thought Jakob had fallen through, there was no sign of him.

"Jakob!" she screamed. "Jakob!"

All was silent.

"Jakob!" she cried again, desperate.

There was a wild thrashing off to her left, and Jakob's head broke through the moss. "Grab the branch!" she told him. "Pull yourself! I'll help!"

Jakob's flailing hands found the branch, and he held it for a moment, gasping. Then he began to pull himself up. Lizzie held the branch steady with all her might, to keep it from sliding below the moss.

"It's holding me," Jakob wheezed. Most of his torso was out of the water. "It's holding my legs!"

Lizzie sat on the branch and reached past it, grabbing the waistband of Jakob's trousers. She yanked as hard as she could. There was a ghastly sucking noise, and Jakob, suddenly released, rocketed upward, knocking Lizzie off the branch onto her back.

For a few minutes they lay on the soft, damp moss, panting. Then Lizzie sat up. She could see that the legs of Jakob's trousers were shredded.

"What *was* that?" she asked him.

He shook his head. "I don't know. I don't want to know. It wanted to pull me under. It had claws, or teeth. Or both."

It was a little while before Jakob was ready to move forward again. Now they walked very cautiously. Jakob carried the branch Lizzie had found, and he used it to test each step to be sure it was on solid ground.

Before long, the ground began to dry, and the moss gave way to a grove of pines. Jakob and Lizzie halted in astonishment. They were like no trees they'd ever seen, their trunks bowed out in a curve near the bottom, all in the same direction. The entire stand of pines looked as if they were kneeling at prayer.

"How did they grow that way?" Lizzie asked.

"I have no idea." Jakob walked forward and picked up a pinecone. Then, with the sharp knife he always carried, he split the branch he carried at its top and stuffed the pinecone into the split. He pulled a kerchief from his pocket and wound it around the split.

"What are you doing?" Lizzie asked.

"Making a torch." He walked up to one of the trees and ran his hand down it. "Ah," he said. "Pitch." He rubbed the kerchief in the pitch, moving from tree to tree so he could coat the cloth thickly with the flammable tree sap. Then he laid the branch on the ground.

"I need a rock," he said. Lizzie looked around. There were plenty of rocks. She picked up a medium-sized one and handed it to him. Kneeling above the torch, he struck his knife against the rock, over and over again. Finally a spark flew onto the pitch-soaked fabric. Lizzie held her breath. The torch ignited with a *whoosh*.

"There we go," Jakob said, pleased. He lifted the torch and held it in front of himself. The kneeling trees looked even stranger in its flickering light.

Then Lizzie noticed his legs. In the torchlight,

she could see that they were striped with deep, thick scratches from knee to ankle. Blood dampened his boots.

"Jakob!" she gasped. "What did that creature do to you?"

Jakob looked down. "It had claws," he said again, his voice a little shaky. "Come on, we're losing precious time."

It was much easier now that they could see the path clearly. Oak trees took over from the congregation of kneeling pines, and the farther in they walked, the more enormous the oaks they passed. Lizzie began to feel tired, but it was hard to measure the passing of time in that gloomy place. How long was it since they'd entered the forest?

"How far in should we go?" Lizzie wondered. "How will we know if this is the right place?"

"It is the right place," a voice ahead of them said.

It was a voice without a color.

Emil's voice.

Lizzie's heart leapt as Emil stepped out of the darkness. He held a torch with a flame that wavered, though the forest air was still as death. Beside him was Minka.

"Minka!" Lizzie cried. "Oh, are you all right?"

"Of course I am," Minka said. "I'm so glad you're here! Now everything will be perfect!"

"Perfect," Emil repeated. He smiled at Lizzie, then deliberately leaned over and kissed Minka. Lizzie shuddered, but Minka's face glowed. Lizzie glanced at Jakob: he was gazing at Minka, his eyes focused on her. It was clear that he didn't see Emil.

Lizzie squinted at Emil. She remembered the moment from their first meeting when she thought she had seen something else where he stood. Something different. The torchlight flickered, and for second Emil seemed to flicker, too. In that instant, she saw the creature she'd almost seen before: sharp teeth, eyes that glowed red.

And then he was handsome Emil again.

She grabbed Jakob's shoulder. "Don't say anything," she whispered. "Don't make him mad."

"No, don't make me mad," Emil agreed. His hearing was far too keen to be human—Lizzie was sure of it. "There's no need for anyone to be upset. We're only here because Minka wanted to see you, Lizzie. The suitor can go."

"He's not going anywhere," Lizzie said defiantly. "And neither is Minka."

"No, we're staying here," Jakob agreed. He was

trying to follow a one-sided conversation, Lizzie knew. He only heard what she said.

Emil laughed. "The suitor's bruise is healing nicely," he said to Lizzie, and she scowled.

"Did you hear that, Minka?" she said. "He's talking about when he hit Jakob. When he *hit* him."

Minka frowned. "You didn't do that, did you, Emil?" she asked. "You wouldn't."

"I never touched him, I swear," Emil said. "Did I, Lizzie?"

He was telling the truth. He hadn't touched Jakob–but somehow he'd bruised him. "You know you did," Lizzie insisted.

"Oh, Lizzie," Minka said. "Stop, please. Can't you see that he makes me happy? Don't you want me to be happy?" She put up a hand and touched Emil gently on the cheek. Lizzie winced.

"Of course I do," she said uncertainly.

"Then come and celebrate with us!"

"Come where?" Lizzie asked.

"Come to my house," Emil said. "It's a beautiful house. It's stone and wood, with a big front porch. There are rockers on the porch, and climbing roses that scent the air when the breeze blows through the windows." His voice grew mesmerizing, almost hypnotic. "Inside, it's bright and clean. There's a room that's just for you, Minka, filled with sunlight, with an easel for your painting. You can hear the babbling of the stream from every room. And behind the house is my orchard, where my fruits grow. Do you remember my fruits, Minka my love? Do you remember?"

Lizzie could picture the house, the orchard, perfectly. It seemed so familiar...

It *was* familiar. Lizzie remembered now.

It was the house Minka had always described to her, when she talked about growing up and having a family of her own. A little wood-and-stone house with a big front porch and an orchard behind and a studio just for art: it was Minka's own imagining. Her own desire. She had even painted it, on the wall in the loft where she could see it before she slept. Had she told Emil—or had he just somehow known?

"Oh," Minka breathed. Her eyes were half closed as she imagined the house of her dreams. "Yes, I want to see your house. It sounds just the way I described my dream house to you last night."

Lizzie blinked when she said that. Last night? But Minka had been home then. How had she spoken to Emil?

The cherry tree. The tree that spoke with Emil's voice. Oh, she should have chopped it down!

"Is there really a room just for me in the house?" Minka asked.

"Just for you," Emil promised. "Even I won't come in—unless you invite me."

Minka smiled up at him. "You can come in anytime you want." She put out her hand, and he took it.

Lizzie felt a scream rising ocher in her chest, and she shouted, *"No!"* as loudly as she could.

Minka turned to her. Her eyes were cold. "You needn't go with us if you don't want to," she said. "You've been invited. But you needn't go."

As Lizzie and Jakob watched in dismay, Minka and Emil started off, deeper into the forest, hand in hand. In a moment the glimmering light of Emil's torch was gone.

CHAPTER 12

"**F**ollow them!" Lizzie cried. She started forward, Jakob following. In a minute, though, the path they were on split and then split again. Lizzie stopped, confused.

"Which way?" Jakob asked.

"Give me a minute," Lizzie said. She looked down one path, then the other. There was just a tinge of rose hovering over the left-hand fork. "This one!" she said. At the next fork she did the same thing. This time they veered right.

"How do you know?" Jakob panted as they hurried along.

"I see the pinkness of Minka's voice," Lizzie said.

Jakob choked, coughing so hard that they had to stop for a moment so he could catch his breath.

"You do what?" he managed.

"I see Minka's voice," Lizzie repeated. "It's pink, mostly."

In the torchlight, Lizzie could see Jakob staring at her. He blinked once or twice and opened his mouth to speak, but finally he nodded. "All right, then. Let's keep on."

The path narrowed still more. They went slowly, stepping over tree limbs that seemed determined to trip them, dodging brambles that reached out to snag them. The silence was oppressive.

"Lizzie," Jakob said after a time, "do you really see . . . the *color* of Minka's voice?"

"Yes," Lizzie said. "And the colors of other voices. And other sounds, too. Rain. A cow mooing. Fire crackling."

"All the time?" Jakob said. "And you never told anyone?"

"Just Minka," Lizzie replied. Then she drew up short, so suddenly that Jakob bumped into her, pushing her over into a thicket of sharp-thorned bushes. The path ended there. It was just gone.

"Ouch, ouch, ouch," Lizzie said, trying to scramble out of the brambles. Jakob helped her up, and she pulled her skirt free of the thorns, hearing the fabric rip.

"Which way now?" Jakob asked. Sweat beaded on his face, and he was breathing heavily.

"I–I'm not sure," Lizzie admitted. She peered ahead into the gloom. There was no puff of pink to trace Minka's steps, no crushed leaves or broken twigs to show which way she and Emil had gone.

"Listen," Jakob said. They held their breaths, and in the utter silence, they could hear a faraway sound off to their left. Was it voices?

She squinted ahead, trying to see if there were any voice-colors hanging in the air. Nothing showed but the vague outline of tree branches in the darkness. That wasn't necessarily because there were no voices ahead, Lizzie knew. It could be because Emil's voice–zduszes' voices–had no color. If it was him they were hearing, or his people, there would be nothing to see.

Moving carefully, picking their way through the underbrush, they headed toward the noise. After a few minutes Jakob, now in the lead, held up a hand. They listened again. Now the voices were on their right.

Over and over, they headed toward the sound, only to find that it had changed location. Lizzie felt as if they'd walked for a dozen miles.

At their next stop, when they heard the bewildering far-off hum to their right, Jakob said, "If we can't find them when we go toward them, we should go the other way."

Lizzie looked at him, confused, but then she nodded. It had a certain uncanny logic to it.

It turned out Jakob was right. They went left, and suddenly, with only a single step forward, Lizzie found herself at the edge of a clearing.

A lush lawn, green-black in the light of a full moon, was ringed with torches. At its far edge was a dark building, and at its center was a long, narrow trestle table with a white cloth over it. Carved wooden benches had been placed along the table. It was set with golden plates and silver utensils; there was a crystal wineglass at each place, and a series of golden candelabra down the center. The candles were lighted.

"Oh!" she breathed.

"What on earth . . . ?" Jakob said.

Lizzie turned her gaze to the structure at the end of the lawn. Her eyes widened in shock. It was the house—Emil's house, Minka's house. It looked exactly as Emil had described it, as Minka had painted it. Flowers twined up the porch railings, and in the light of the moon and the torches, Lizzie made out two rocking chairs.

The chairs weren't empty. There were people sitting in them, both with dark curls like Emil's.

Then a cloud passed in front of the moon and Lizzie gasped.

The light had dimmed, but she could still see what sat in the rockers. They no longer looked entirely human. Their forms wavered, and she could make out sharp claws, tails that switched back and forth with the movement of the chairs. As Lizzie stared in horror, one of the figures looked at her and showed its pointed teeth in a cold smile.

She stumbled backward with a whimper.

"What?" Jakob said. "What's wrong?"

"Do you see anything?" Lizzie asked him in a whisper. "Tell me what you see."

"There's a table, and torches, and a house," Jakob said. "A little house, with a front porch. Chairs rocking in the breeze."

"You don't see...them?" Lizzie asked.

"No."

Lizzie looked again. The cloud passed and the moon was uncovered. Now the two figures rocking back and forth were a woman and a man.

"There are two creatures sitting in the chairs,"

Lizzie whispered. "I don't know what they are. They look like people, and then they don't."

"Why don't I see them?" Jakob asked, frustrated.

Lizzie had been wondering this since Jakob's encounter with Emil at the market. She thought she had the answer. "That's how it goes in the old stories—it's children or girls who see them. Sometimes they're in their goblin form, and sometimes they look like humans."

"I'm a boy, and older," Jakob said slowly. "So I don't see them at all?"

"Right."

Jakob peered toward the house and shook his head. "I'd say that makes sense, but none of this does. What do they look like?"

"I can't really tell. They have sharp teeth. And tails, I think."

Jakob grimaced. "Come on," he said. He started across the lawn, and Lizzie followed.

As they crossed the wide expanse of grass, Lizzie felt horribly exposed. The pair on the front porch watched them with great interest. As they neared, Lizzie could see that the woman, like Emil, was astonishingly beautiful. Her long, dark hair cascaded over her shoulders nearly to her waist; her lips were full and lush, her eyes large and luminous. The man in the rocker beside her looked like Emil, only older, and even more handsome. His father, uncle? Older brother? Both watched Lizzie with small, slight smiles. Lizzie had to remind herself of what lay beneath their lovely exteriors—the red eyes, the tails, the pointed teeth.

Lizzie and Jakob reached the porch steps and looked up at the couple in the chairs, who regarded them with amusement.

"Is my sister in there?" It took all Lizzie's courage to ask the question.

The woman tilted her head. "Why, I don't know, Elzbieta. Who is your sister?" Her words were colorless.

"Minka," Lizzie said. "If you know who I am, you know who she is. Is she there? Do you have her?"

The man pursed his lips. "*Have* her? What a strange thing to say."

Lizzie was getting angry, and the anger replaced some of the fear that made her knees weak. She leapt up the steps, strode over to the front door, and tried to turn the knob. It was locked. "Let me in. I want to go in and get her!" she insisted.

"She is getting ready," the woman said.

"Ready? Ready for what?" Lizzie demanded.

"Why, for the wedding, of course," the woman replied, her voice silky-smooth.

"The *wedding*?" Behind her, Lizzie heard Jakob's intake of breath.

"We are all here for the wedding," the woman said. She gestured with her arm, and Lizzie followed the movement with her eyes.

From the trees that ringed the lawn, figures appeared. They looked human. They wore beautiful, sumptuous clothing—embroidered vests and skirts, bright striped trousers, tall hats with ribbons and tassels on them. Exactly what people going to a wedding might wear if they dressed in their finest.

As Lizzie watched in horror, the group—there must have been thirty of them, or more—walked slowly across the lawn and took their seats at the table, leaving the head and foot empty. They raised their goblets in a silent toast.

"What is it? What's happening?" Jakob hissed.

"There are so many of them," Lizzie said faintly. "They're all sitting down at the table."

Jakob reached for her hand, and she let him take it as she watched. Two more figures came out from the trees and walked to the table, one carrying a rosebush in a golden pot, the other a thornbush in a silver pot. They placed the rose at one end of the table and the thorn at the far end.

From behind the house, a group of five came onto the lawn. They carried musical instruments. There were a fiddler, a flute player, a big double bass. A man with no instrument. They tuned up, and the sound of their music had no color. Then the one without an instrument stepped forward and began to sing a melancholy tune in a minor key:

> *"Love is love, but whom love swayeth*
> *Pays love's price and love betrayeth.*
> *I, unwise, love's price have given,*
> *Head and heart with pain are riven."*

Lizzie was lost in the song. It went on, stanza after stanza of heartache, suffering, despair. Lovers lost each other, died, ran away, were betrayed. It was unbearably sad. Lizzie pulled her hand from Jakob's to wipe her eyes. Why would anyone sing such a song at a wedding?

"Lizzie!" Jakob's voice drew her out of the reverie the song had created. "We have to go in. We have to find Minka!"

Minka. Yes. They were here for Minka. Somehow, she had nearly forgotten.

"Who is this boy?" the goblin man on the porch asked. "What does he want?"

"He's Jakob. He wants the same thing I do—my sister. To take her home."

"But she is home," the woman said. "This is her house now."

"Jakob is a handsome lad," the man mused. "Perhaps he should stay. Perhaps you both should stay. We can find you each someone to marry!"

"Stay here?" Lizzie said. "No. None of us will stay. Jakob knows what you are, and so do I." She turned to Jakob. He was staring at the rocking chairs, blinking hard.

"That's right," the woman said to him in a lilting, teasing tone. "Open your eyes. Look at us. Look carefully. Now you can hear us, now you can see us, can't you? *Aren't we lovely?*"

The man laughed. "He thinks we are! Now he understands, don't you, Jakob? Do you want to stay? Will you eat our fruit, make us a promise, let us give you your heart's desire? *Stay!*"

Jakob gave Lizzie a frantic, horrified look.

"They're not what they seem, you know that!" Lizzie cried. "Squint your eyes and look at them again, Jakob! Look hard!"

The woman hissed as Jakob did what Lizzie said. His eyes suddenly cleared, and he inhaled sharply and stepped back, nearly falling down the porch steps.

"Oh," he said faintly.

"That's right," Lizzie said. "Don't forget it. That's what they are. Now, come on!" She turned to the woman on the porch again. "I want to go in to see my sister," she said firmly.

"Ah, why didn't you say so?" The woman stood, leaving the chair rocking gently. "Of course, come in, come in." She turned the knob that had been locked when Lizzie tried it. The green wooden front door swung open easily, and the woman gestured for Lizzie to enter. Lizzie stepped into the house.

The door slammed behind her.

She spun around. It was dark in the room where she stood, the only light a faint moonglow through a window on her right. She tried to pull open the door, but it wouldn't budge.

"Jakob!" she cried. "Jakob!" She listened for his reply.

Nothing.

She hammered on the door, yanked at it, kicked it. Oh, she didn't want to be alone in this house! But there was no sound, inside or out.

She couldn't leave. She could only go on.

She turned back into the room. If her memory of Minka's description served her, this was the parlor. Beside it was a kitchen, and behind, in the back of the house, would be the bedroom and Minka's painting studio. She walked forward carefully, her hands outstretched, afraid she'd trip over a piece of furniture or bang into a wall. No color came from the sound of her feet scraping across the wood floor.

When she reached the far wall, she felt along it for a doorway. Ah, there! A latch that could be lifted. She pushed it upward and pulled the door open. But the room it opened onto wasn't the studio, as she had expected. She could see a little more clearly; one of the torches from outside cast light through a window.

There were odd bundles on the floor, a dozen or more. She walked up to one of them. It was brownish green, like the leaf of a huge plant, wrapped tightly around something to make a packet. From each packet, a slight whimpering emerged.

Cautiously, she stretched out her hand, and gently, gently, she pulled the bundle open.

Lying in the leaf as if in swaddling clothes was an infant. A beautiful baby, pink-cheeked and sleeping. Was it a stolen child? Lizzie couldn't help herself; she touched the baby on its soft cheek.

It opened its eyes. They were red. It opened its delicate rosebud mouth, showing sharp yellow teeth. And then it shrieked, a piercing howl that had no color.

Lizzie screamed, too, backing away as fast as she could, her hands over her ears. This was a nursery. A zdusze nursery, filled with goblin babies. She tripped over her own feet, falling on her tailbone and scrambling up quickly. The other leaf-packets were rolling back and forth now; the whimpering had grown louder. The babies were waking up.

Lizzie ran for the nearest door, opposite the one she'd come in. She threw it open and darted into the next room, slamming the door behind her. Her heart hammered as she tried to catch her breath.

She was in a kitchen. There were two huge iron stoves, where figures stood and stirred bubbling pots. At a long counter, others chopped objects Lizzie couldn't identify. A tiered, frosted cake stood on a table. Lizzie crept to a door just beyond the table, glancing at the cake as she passed. Flowers adorned the layers, but the blooms were dead and crumbling. The smells that rose from the stove made Lizzie gag. As one, the cooks turned to stare at her, and the nearest held out an iron spoon.

"Taste!" she invited. A dark, viscous liquid dripped onto the floor. Swiftly, Lizzie opened the door and slipped through.

The door led to a room that held only an enormous claw-footed bathtub. As Lizzie started to move past it, the toes on the tub's claw feet seemed to wriggle and twitch. Then, as if they were fingers, they started to pull the tub across the floor toward her. She reached the bathtub room's nearest door, but when she paused, she could hear noises from inside. Groans, growls. A keening voice rose up, wailing. It seemed to call to her, to beg her for help. But it had no color, and she knew it was a goblin voice. She turned to see the tub, moving fast now as the claw feet scrabbled on the wood, careening toward her. Leaping out of the way, she pushed through the third door in the bathroom as the tub crashed into the wall where she'd been standing, denting the whitewashed wood.

Lizzie found herself in a space that was dim and green. Squinting, she tried to make out the shapes that lined the walls and ceiling. Ah, they were plants! The whole room was filled with plants. Above one of them a fly buzzed, and she watched in revulsion as the plant's stem stretched upward and a protuberance reached out and snapped on the fly like jaws.

On the far side of the room, she could see a door, and she moved toward it. The leaves on the plants were swaying, though no breeze blew. One stem extended itself toward her, its leafy jaws gnashing. She tried to duck under it, but it was quick, and its thin, brittle teeth met on her arm. She pulled back with a cry, and the stem withdrew. The teeth were as sharp as a knife blade. They had sliced right through her sleeve and cut her arm, just as the plum tree branch had. Blood welled up, and she dabbed at it with her torn sleeve.

How could this little house have so many rooms? From the outside it seemed not much larger than her own cottage. It should have had space only for a parlor, a kitchen, a bedroom, and a loft, like hers. And the studio, of course. She was completely disoriented. Which way had she come? How would she get out?

The next door opened on an empty room—no furnishings, no curtains at the windows. Just a carpet. A carpet that...moved.

A carpet of snakes. Dozens, maybe hundreds of snakes.

Lizzie had never been afraid of snakes, not like Jakob was, or Minka. She picked up garter snakes crossing the lane and helped them to safety without thinking twice; she watched green grass snakes slither through the fields and admired their grace. But these weren't harmless grass snakes; they were enormous. They had fangs. They hissed. For the first time since she'd entered the house, she was very glad Jakob wasn't with her. He would have fainted with terror. And Minka—had she passed through this room? Had she been frightened?

Lizzie pulled the door nearly closed again so the snakes wouldn't slither out, using her boot to keep it open. She peered through the narrow opening. The only other door was on the far side of the room. She either had to go back or go through. And if she went back, she'd never find Minka.

Maybe they're not real, she thought. But then one struck at her boot, and she felt the jolt of it. It was as real as the goblins were. Her mind worked frantically to figure out a way across the room.

Speed—that was her only hope. If she ran as fast as she could, maybe the snakes couldn't strike her quickly enough. But if she fell...Before she could talk herself out of it, she shoved the door all the way open, pushing the snakes aside, and leapt into the room. It was only a few meters to the other side. One of her feet landed on a snake body, and she nearly lost her balance as it writhed beneath her boot. She raced forward, reaching for the door on the far side.

But it wasn't there.

The room had somehow lengthened, and now the door looked distant—as if it were down a long hall.

But there were snakes ahead of her and snakes behind. She had to keep running.

As serpents raised their long bodies up, prepared to strike, she dodged and wove through them, jumping when they lunged at her so their fangs would only hit her boots. Some of them spat; some of them stayed low and tried to bite. Some tried to wind themselves around her legs to trip her. She shook them off, sidestepped them, kicked at them, stamped on them.

She must have run nearly a mile when, head down, she crashed into the closed door she'd been aiming at, nearly knocking herself to the ground. As one huge cobra raised itself up—up as high as her chin!—she threw the door open and dashed through, slamming it just as the serpent struck. The weight of its heavy body made the door shudder behind her. She leaned against it, hands on her knees, gasping for breath. Finally she looked up.

At last, at last, she was in the painting studio.

A flood of light made her blink, trying to adjust her eyes. Easels stood beside long windows framed with sheer white drapes that pooled on the floor. The smell of paint and turpentine was thick, nearly suffocating. Paintings hung on and leaned against the walls. Lizzie looked, appalled, from one canvas to the next. Each was worse than the last, pictures of frightful creatures pulling people beneath the earth, into pools of murky water, into pyres of flame. The images made her stomach churn, and she turned away.

And in the middle of the room was the source of the light: a circle of candles of all sizes and shapes.

Some were tall, some short; some thin, others thick. All were lighted, and the flickering candlelight showed two figures sitting in the center of the circle.

Emil and Minka.

CHAPTER 13

Minka!" Lizzie cried, and her sister turned her head. She looked unsurprised at Lizzie's sudden appearance. Her eyes were glazed and seemed slightly out of focus, as if she were seeing something inside her mind, not what she was looking at.

"Well, Lizzie," she said. "Does this mean you've decided to celebrate with us?" In this space, this evil room, Minka's words appeared to have no color. Was it because she was becoming one of them, one of the zduszes? She clasped Emil's hand in hers, and Emil looked at Lizzie, smiling. In the dancing light, his beautiful face altered, transformed, from boy to creature and back. Lizzie shuddered.

"What...what are you wearing?" Lizzie stared at the couple. Emil had on a long ivory coat and a hat with a peacock feather that trailed over his shoulder. And Minka! She was in an ivory brocade gown sewn thickly with pearls. It was a hundred times fancier than any dress Lizzie had ever seen. And around her neck was the silver locket Emil had given her.

"It's my wedding dress," Minka said proudly. She stood and spun in a circle, her dress swirling around her delicate embroidered shoes. The skirt swung dangerously close to the candle flames.

"Are you—are you really getting married?" Lizzie asked.

"We are!" Minka said. "I *am* glad you decided to come. I didn't want to marry without any of my family."

"I'm not here for that," Lizzie said. "I've come to take you home. You don't belong here. Come back with me. We're all waiting. Mother and Father are waiting. Kosmy is hungry for his dinner." She hoped the mention of the donkey would strike a chord in her sister.

A shadow passed over Minka's face and then cleared. "They'll be fine," she said. "You can take care of Kosmy. I'm staying here."

Lizzie clenched her fists, trying to raise the anger that had given her strength before. "I won't go without you. I won't!"

"Then you stay, too," Emil said. Lizzie stared

as he wavered and shifted before her eyes: human, not-human, human.

"Yes, stay!" Minka cried. "Stay and be my brides-maid. Stay for the wedding. Stay!"

"Stay," Emil echoed. "Stay!"

"I don't want to," Lizzie whispered.

"Oh, Lizzie," Minka said, "don't you want to be with me? You know you do! Here, help me put on my wianek and veil." She rose and stepped out of the circle of candlelight, holding her skirt up away from the flames.

"You aren't supposed to wear pearls at your wedding," Lizzie said. "It brings misery." There must have been hundreds of white pearls on the dress, sewn in flower patterns from hem to waist.

"Oh, they aren't pearls," Emil said, laughter in his voice. Lizzie bent to look more closely.

No, they weren't pearls. They were teeth. Tiny teeth—children's teeth. For a moment Lizzie feared she would be sick.

"Don't frighten her, Emil," Minka scolded. From a table by the wall she lifted a circlet of flowers and rosemary. Lizzie had seen village brides wearing such wreaths as they walked to the church in Elza through a crowd of cheering neighbors. This wianek was woven with bizarre blooms she'd never seen before, though, not the roses and poppies that were customary at home.

Minka held out a delicate embroidered veil to Lizzie. "Put it on me," she commanded. "There's no mirror, so I can't do it myself."

"I don't want to," Lizzie protested. "Minka, please, come home with me!"

"You help me, Emil," Minka said. Emil reached for the veil, but Lizzie snatched it from him.

"I'll do it," she said. She draped the veil over Minka's head. Her sister had no hair to be woven into the traditional braids of a bride, but the veil covered its lack. Then Lizzie took the circlet and placed it atop the veil, holding it in place.

"How do I look?" Minka asked. Lizzie couldn't really see her face through the veil.

"I suppose you look beautiful," she said. "But this is a terrible mistake. Please, Minka!"

There was a silence, and then Minka gave a laugh that sounded forced. "You always do say what you think, Lizzie!"

"Are you ready, my love?" Emil had come up behind them. The sound of his voice made Lizzie jump.

"I am," Minka said. "Lizzie, you walk behind us. We'll walk through the wedding gate, we'll eat the bread and salt, and we'll be married!"

No, no, no, Lizzie thought, but she couldn't think how to stop it. Somehow she had to wake Minka from the trance she seemed to be in, to make her see that Emil was wasn't what he appeared, that his love was false. But she had no plan.

Heartsick, she followed the couple as Emil opened the door to the studio. It was the door Lizzie had entered through, and she was ready to jump back in case the snakes poured in. But instead the door led to the big porch that wrapped around the house.

Nothing in this house made sense.

They walked along the porch, lighted with torches, to the front of the house. The rocking chairs were gone now. Instead, there was an archway of flowers—the wedding gate—and through it Lizzie looked down at the scene on the lawn below. The musicians played a polonaise. The guests had risen from their seats at the table and were dancing in pairs, taking sliding steps up and down the lawn.

As she watched, Lizzie noticed that one of the gorgeous goblin-women was dancing with a partner wearing not a tall hat and long coat but tattered trousers and thick boots–Jakob. He was surprisingly graceful, but every time his hand touched his partner's, he flinched. After a moment he looked up, saw the threesome on the porch, and tried to disentangle himself. The woman clung to his sleeve; he pulled away, and for an instant she seemed to flicker and change in the moonlight to something smaller, not quite opaque, monstrous. With a powerful yank Jakob freed his sleeve and ran to the foot of the steps that led up to the porch.

"Lizzie!" he cried. "I've been so scared–I didn't know what had happened to you! And you found Minka!"

"You were *dancing,*" Lizzie said accusingly.

"It wasn't my choice," Jakob told her, his eyes bright with fear. "I tried to go after you, but those two on the porch–I don't know *what* they did to me. When the dancing started, I had to join in. It was like my feet belonged to someone else."

Emil laughed. "They can be very persuasive, can't they? You are less awkward than I would have guessed, suitor! Perhaps I will allow you to dance with my bride after we are wed."

Jakob clenched his fists and looked back and forth from Minka to Emil. It was clear that he could see Emil now.

"They're going to be married. Now, right now," Lizzie said desperately. She tried to tell Jakob with her eyes that she didn't know what to do. She had never been very good at signaling things with her expression.

But Jakob seemed to understand. He nodded. "That's... wonderful," he said. "But Minka, you can't just walk through the wedding gate, don't you recall? You have to pay a bribe to the groom's family to go through. Remember Balbina's wedding?"

Minka blinked. "Why... yes. I do. That's right. It wasn't a real bribe, though. Not money. She paid in candies, didn't she? But I haven't any candy. I haven't anything at all. I came here with nothing."

"Then the match will be cursed," Jakob said. Lizzie looked at him. Wasn't a match with a goblin already cursed? Maybe he didn't know what he was doing, but at least he might delay things a little.

"We could go home and get something to pay with, me and you," Lizzie suggested. "We could fetch candy, or money—whatever you want." If she could only get Minka home!

"We don't need to hold with that tradition," Emil protested. "Come, my love, we can just walk through, and then we'll be married. Don't pay these fools any mind."

Minka seemed undecided at first, but to Lizzie's dismay, she nodded slowly. "Yes, we have new traditions now, haven't we?" She stroked Emil's arm.

"Wait!" Lizzie cried in desperation. "You do have something to pay with. You do!" Minka looked at her, confused.

"What is that, sister-to-be?" Emil asked, lifting an eyebrow.

"You have me," Lizzie said, looking straight at Minka. "You can go through the wedding gate if you pay with me."

The musicians stopped playing abruptly, and the dancers turned as one to look up at the group on the porch. The silence was sudden and absolute.

Minka's face was blank. "What? What do you mean?"

"Give me to them," Lizzie said fiercely. "If you're staying with them, I am, too."

She hadn't planned to say it. But she meant it. She couldn't leave Minka here alone with these creatures. She just couldn't.

"No, Lizzie!" Jakob protested.

"Interesting," Emil said. "So we would get two sisters for the price of one, so to speak."

"You don't want her," Minka said uncertainly. "She's a child. It's me you love…isn't it?" She looked up at Emil with pleading eyes.

"Oh, darling, of course it is," Emil assured her. "But Lizzie is nearly grown. She can be…of use."

At his words, the rest of the goblin company moved closer, and Lizzie shuddered. "Yes," she said. "I can be of use."

"Yes," Emil said, and the goblins below murmured, "Yessss. Yessss." They began to climb the porch stairs. Lizzie backed away until she was pressed against the wall of the house, and they crowded around her.

One of the zduszes, a man dressed in a long coat embroidered with intricate black-and-red patterns, held out a pear in one hand, a bunch of purple grapes in the other. The scents of the fruit rose and mingled, and, despite her fear and revulsion, Lizzie's mouth watered. Oh, they looked so delicious, so perfect! If she could only taste one grape, one small grape…

The man plucked a grape and held it up near Lizzie's mouth. She followed the movement hungrily with her eyes, opened her lips just a little.

"Taste!" a woman urged her. "One little taste! Stay with us, stay with your sister. You know you want to!"

The man pushed the grape against Lizzie's mouth—but she clamped her lips shut. "Taste, taste!" he insisted. He pressed the grape against her lips until the juice from it ran down her chin, but she kept her mouth closed.

"Taste!" the goblin-woman repeated. She held up a ripe dark fruit and waved it under Lizzie's nose. Lizzie turned away from the scent, and the goblin crushed the fruit in her hand and smeared it on Lizzie's cheeks. "This is a perfect fig. Taste! You will never have another chance, you will never eat anything more wondrous in your life. If you want to stay, you must eat!"

Another creature joined them, a graceful man who moved a little like a cat, with ears that twitched back and forth. He pressed a peach, dripping with nectar, against Lizzie's lips. "So few have the good fortune to try our fruits," he murmured in her ear. "You are chosen, you are one of the special ones!"

Their voices were as sweet as their fruits smelled—but they had no color. Every word reminded Lizzie of what they were, of what they wanted. The juices from their fruits ran down her neck, soaking her blouse, and she crouched against the porch wall, her hand covering her mouth, to get away from them, to keep even one drop of the juice from leaking through her lips.

The zduszes began to grow angry. They crowded around Lizzie, jostling her and poking at her with sharp claws. "Taste!" they insisted. "Don't be so proud, so stubborn! Taste, stay, be one of us!" They were snarling now, their honeyed tones turning low and harsh.

"Leave her alone!" Jakob cried. But he couldn't get to Lizzie through the crowd of creatures.

Terrified, Lizzie shook her head, closing her eyes against the goblins' wrath. One tore at her skirt, one pulled her hair, the catlike goblin pelted her with cherries as she knelt on the floor with her hands over her face. "If you don't eat, you cannot be one of us. You must eat if you want to stay with your sister!"

She knew it was true. She had offered herself, but she had to eat the fruit to be with Minka. She raised her head, ready to open her mouth.

"Stop! Stop it!" she heard through the cacophony of goblin hisses and mewls. It was Minka's voice, clear and forceful. "Leave her alone! What are you doing?"

"We're doing what you want us to do," Lizzie heard Emil say. "We are getting your dear sister to stay with us."

"Stop!" cried Minka. "You're tormenting her! That's not what I want, not at all!"

"No?" said Emil.

"No?" the others echoed.

"Whatever do you mean by 'stop'?" Emil demanded. "You have said yes all along! It has been yes, and yes, and yes with you!"

Lizzie opened her eyes, blinking with the sting of the fruit juices, to see Minka trying to push through the crowd to get to her.

"I was wrong," Minka said.

As Lizzie watched, Emil's beautiful curls transmuted into a bald, wrinkled scalp; his dark eyes flashed red; his perfect mouth opened to reveal a mouthful of jagged yellow teeth. Did Minka see how he changed? Or did he still look like a handsome boy to her?

"I was wrong about you," Minka said, slowly. "You're not what I thought, not at all. You're not what I want."

"Don't be absurd," Emil said, changing back into his boy-self before Lizzie's eyes. His flawless brow was furrowed with a frown. In the torchlight Lizzie could see an expression of sorrow on his face. Was it real? Emil reached out a hand and caressed Minka's arm. "Darling Minka, precious Minka, I am everything you want. You know I am. It is and will always be the two of us. *Emil and Minka, me and you. Emil and Minka, just we two.*"

Lizzie stared at him, shocked beyond words.

How *dare* he quote the lines from the song she and Minka had invented, their song of sisterhood? It was theirs and theirs alone. She looked at Minka, bewildered. Would Minka have betrayed her by telling him about it?

But no. Minka was as startled as Lizzie. Not just startled—angry.

"How did you know those lines from our song?" she demanded.

Emil waved a hand as if brushing away her question. But she stamped a foot and repeated, "How did you know?" The goblins seemed to like her foot-stamping. They all pounded their feet on the porch floor. It shook beneath them.

"Why, through our tree, dearest!" Emil told her.

"Our tree? Our cherry tree? But—you spied on us with it? You listened to me talking to Lizzie? I thought the tree was just—just for you and me!" Lizzie could see the color rising in Minka's voice, growing stronger and darker. "That is not the way the song goes, Emil. It's not you and me, it's me and my sister—Lizzie and Minka. It's not your song to sing." Minka took a deep breath. Then she said, "And I'm not yours, either."

Emil narrowed his eyes and showed his sharp teeth. "But you *are* mine. You're here, in my home. You've given me a lock of your hair; you've eaten my fruit. Your choice is not whether to stay or go, but whether your sister stays with you or goes."

Minka stepped closer to Lizzie and reached out to clasp her hand. "I'm not yours if I decide not to be," she said to Emil. "It's my choice, whether I've eaten your fruit or not." Her voice grew angrier. "And how could you think that I wanted to be parted from Lizzie?" she cried. "*You* didn't want her here. *You* made it hard for her to find us. *You* set traps for her. I know you did! But she is too smart for you." She squeezed Lizzie's hand. "Nobody should ever want to tear two sisters apart—nobody human! I love Lizzie, and she loves me. Her love is real—it's not like yours. She was right. I see it now. You are a zdusze. You're not human, not at all. And you can't have my sister!"

Lizzie was struck by her words. *Her love is real—it's not like yours.* She recalled what the prorok had said: *You must try to fight him with his own weapon. Yours is real; his is not.*

Had she been talking about love? Was her weapon her love for her sister?

"Minka, I do love you," she cried out. "I love you!"

Emil hissed and gnashed his discolored teeth. Any doubt Lizzie had had about whether Minka could see him in this form was gone, for Minka shrank from him and from the hairless claw he stretched out toward her.

"You will stay," he threatened.

Minka shook her head. "No," she said. Her voice was a tentative puff of pale pink.

"You *must* stay," Emil insisted.

"No!" This time, a swirl of dark magenta rose above the torchlight, a strong color for a strong voice.

Emil reached out for Minka again. She dodged away, knocking against one of the other goblins, who stumbled into a torch. Flames leapt onto the creature's skirt, and it let out a howl of terror. It opened the door to the house and fled inside.

Lizzie seized the moment. She tightened her grip on Minka's hand and sprang forward, pulling her sister around, not through, the wedding gate. "Run!" she cried. "Run!"

The goblins clutched at them, trying to stop them from leaping off the porch. But they fought free of the grasping hands just as an enormous *whoosh* that almost blinded Lizzie with vermillion came from inside.

They spun and saw the curtains at the nearest window shoot up in flame. In just a moment the whole room behind them was afire. The goblins shrieked and scattered, trying to push Lizzie and Minka aside to flee down the stairs. The house was quickly engulfed in flames.

Jakob rushed up the steps, shoving through fleeing zduszes as he made his way to the sisters. He lunged forward, grabbed Lizzie with one arm and Minka with the other, and hauled them down the stairs as the ceiling of the blazing house crashed in behind them. The sound was an intense wave of maroon; the heat from the collapse washed over them. They stumbled to the lawn and ran across it— past the long table with its elegant, abandoned place settings, past the screeching band, past the fleeing goblins—until they were a safe distance from the house. Then they turned back.

Flames shot high into the sky, and smoke billowed upward, darker than the night. Lizzie had never seen a fire devour a building like that, not even when their neighbor Vitold's barn had burned one dry May after a lightning strike. This fire blazed not only orange and red but blue and green in its intense heat. Lizzie and Minka clung together as they watched the flames consume the house, so quickly that it seemed only minutes had passed before the rest of the roof collapsed and only the stone shell of the structure remained.

CHAPTER 14

When the crackling of the flames had settled to a hiss, with an occasional crash as a remaining piece of wall or a part of the chimney buckled, Jakob said, "Minka, are you all right?"

Minka took a long, shuddery breath. "I don't know," she said. But to Lizzie she sounded more like herself than she had in weeks. She pulled off her veil and flower crown and threw them down. Then she tore at the bodice of her dress, the horrid wedding dress, with her fingernails.

"Help me, please," she said to Lizzie. "I can't stand wearing this for another minute, I can't!"

Lizzie started to unbutton the bodice, but when she remembered that each button was a child's tooth, she found she couldn't bear to touch them. She grasped the top of the dress and yanked hard, and the tooth-buttons popped off. As Jakob turned away politely, Minka shrugged out of the bodice, then stepped out of the skirt and kicked it as far as she could.

"Turn around and don't be silly, Jakob," Minka scolded. "I have my chemise and underskirt on. I'm wearing more than Lizzie is!"

"We should get out of here before the zduszes come for us," Lizzie said.

Jakob grabbed one of the torches that lined the goblins' lawn, and they hurried back into the forest, Minka and Jakob together, Lizzie behind them.

"I'm sorry," Minka said, low, as they walked as quickly as they could. "I put you both in danger because of my stupidity. I'm really, really sorry."

"It wasn't your fault," Jakob said, lighting the way with the brand. "He wasn't a person. He was a goblin."

"But I should have known," Minka said. "How could I have been so wrong? I should have seen it. I was—I was—"

"Human," Jakob finished for her.

"I don't know," Minka said. "I felt like I was in a dream, most of the time. Ever since I ate the plum, really. Or, like everything—*you*—were the dream, and the only waking part, the only *real* part, was Emil. His voice, his face, were the only clear things."

"He used some kind of evil magic, that's obvious,"

Jakob said. "If he hadn't, you wouldn't have been fooled."

"I might have. It wasn't just magic. He offered me things…"

"What things?"

Minka sighed. "Love."

Lizzie could see Jakob wince as she walked behind them.

"That wasn't real. None of it was real. I can see that now," Minka went on. "He wasn't who he said he was, and he…he didn't really love me. But it wasn't just love I wanted. What he promised—it sounded like…freedom. To do what I wanted to do. To be who I wanted to be. He knew I wanted more than I had. He saw that right away."

"And he preyed on it," Jakob pointed out. "He told you exactly what you wanted to hear."

"I would have *married* him," Minka said in a shaky voice. "What kind of horror would that have been?"

"Don't think about it," Lizzie advised.

"I can't help it. I have to. I have to figure out why I went with him."

"You didn't do anything wrong!" Lizzie protested.

"No?" Minka laughed harshly. "Lizzie, I would

have left you all–I would have done *anything*–for a goblin. A zdusze! Why didn't I see him for what he was?"

Jakob reached for her hand and gave it a squeeze. "I did the same thing, for a few minutes. They showed themselves to me, Minka. The goblins. And they were...bewitching. They promised so much. Everyone sees what they want to see in certain people. It's just that usually, the person they're looking at isn't–well, isn't a goblin!"

Minka laughed again. This time there were tears in her voice. Lizzie's heart hurt to hear it.

It was only a few minutes later that Lizzie noticed a sound. A color. A light puff of purple off to their left. No, four puffs that rose and dissipated in the wavering lantern light. Then another four, and another. Something was walking alongside them–something with four feet.

"I think there are wolves," she whispered. "Keep walking."

Jakob stumbled slightly, then tightened his grip on Minka. "Where?" he whispered back.

"On our left. At least two." Lizzie could see more purplish puffs now as the wolves paced beside them, just out of the light.

They walked faster, but the wolves kept up, and then the purple footpads moved in front of them. Minka gave a cry of fear as Jakob stopped abruptly, the torchlight showing two sleek gray bodies ahead in their path. Lizzie spun to run back the way they'd come, but there were three other wolves behind them.

They were surrounded.

Lizzie stood back-to-back with Jakob and Minka, facing the way they'd come as the others faced forward. The wolves paced slowly, their long tails swinging, pulling up their lips to show sharp teeth, yellow in the moonlight. Lizzie could feel Minka trembling against her, but Jakob stood staunch.

"I have my knife, if they attack," he murmured. Lizzie shook her head. What good would a single knife do against five wolves? "Wolves don't like noise. If we need to, make yourself big, wave your arms, make a racket. Don't take your eyes off them. And *don't run*."

One of the wolves growled, and the growl became a high-pitched howl that echoed through the trees. The sound was an intense bloodred purple, a color that in Minka's paint box was labeled SUGAR PLUM. Such a sweet name for such a terrifying color! The other wolves joined in, and Lizzie watched as the zigzag lines of color swirled and merged and disappeared into the forest canopy. And then she noticed something peculiar.

One of the wolves she was facing was howling with the others, but its howl had no color.

She turned her head and looked at the wolves in front. One of them howled purple red. The other—no color. No color at all.

Two of the wolves were zduszes.

"Jakob, pass me your knife," she hissed.

He shook his head. "Too dangerous. Too many of them."

"Give it here! I won't use it on a wolf."

With as few movements as possible, Jakob slid the blade from its leather sheath at his waist. He passed it back to Lizzie.

"Do what I say," Lizzie whispered to Minka. "When I jump, you yell and wave your arms. Yell as loud as you can."

Keeping her eyes on the two real wolves in front of her, Lizzie noted the position of the zdusze-wolf beside them with a sidelong glance. She took a deep breath—and then leapt, bringing the knife down onto the zdusze's snout.

Minka let out an earsplitting shriek and waved her arms wildly, right on cue, and Lizzie shouted along with her. Jakob, catching on, roared.

The goblin-wolf twisted and yowled. Its wolf-snout spouted blood. The real wolves backed away from the loud noise and sudden movements, but like Lizzie, they were drawn to watch the zdusze as it writhed and metamorphosed, its sleek gray body shortening and lightening, its hair darkening and curling. For a moment, it looked like a person, its face covered with blood.

"Emil!" Minka wailed.

And then there was silence, and Lizzie saw Emil look at Minka. In the torchlight, his gaze was intense, and Lizzie thought she could see something almost human—regret? sorrow?—in it. The zdusze changed again, flickering as Lizzie had seen it do before. Red eyes, long sharp teeth, a naked tail. The wavering suggestion of an animal form. Minka sank into a crouch, covering her eyes.

The real wolves growled. Lizzie dared a look at the two ahead of them and could see that the second goblin-wolf had changed shape, too. For a moment it looked human; then it shifted into another shape, something shadowy and menacing. The real wolves bared their teeth again, but this time they were looking at the zduszes as they growled.

The goblins backed away slowly as the wolves advanced on them. Lizzie heard a shriek, a snarl, the snap of breaking branches. A sudden wind extinguished their torch and blew a cloud across the moon, plunging the forest into darkness.

They huddled together in the dark, Lizzie's arms tightly around Minka, as the noises from the wolves chasing—and then eating?—the zduszes faded gradually into the distance. When the moon showed itself again, Lizzie helped Minka rise to standing.

"I thought you weren't going to stab a wolf," Jakob said.

"I didn't. I stabbed a zdusze."

"Right," Jakob said. "Good for you." Lizzie handed the knife back to Jakob, and he bent to clean it on the grass and then put it back in its sheath.

"I made it bleed," Lizzie said, shivering at the memory of Emil's bloody face. Minka gave a little whimper, then was quiet.

Eventually they began moving again, stumbling along what they hoped was a path, stopping to listen for footpads or howls or snarls in the underbrush. They moved step by cautious step, grasping each other's arms, and still they tripped over branches and were scratched by brambles. All was blessedly quiet, but Lizzie had no idea if they were going in the right direction.

It seemed as if hours had passed when Jakob stopped abruptly. "Look! What's that?"

Lizzie saw a light flickering amid the trees, and her heart gave a lurching, frightened leap in her chest.

"Oh no," she whispered. "They're back."

"Listen!" Minka held up a hand.

In the distance, Lizzie heard a call: "Lizzie! Minka! Where are you?"

"Is it the goblins again?" Minka quavered. She clutched Lizzie's arm tightly.

"Wait," Lizzie said. She peered into the trees, where the light danced.

"Minka! Jakob!" Lizzie could imagine the goblins masquerading as people, people they knew, and calling their names to try to fool them. That was just what they'd do. But no—there was a puff of aquamarine illuminated by the glimmering light. The blue-green color of a beloved voice.

"It's Mother!" Lizzie cried. "Oh, it's Mother!"

The three of them broke ranks and ran forward. In

a minute they could see that the glow was of torches, and the torches were held by familiar hands: Father, Mother, Mistress Klara. Stefan and Dr. Śmigly. And behind them, Jakob's father, red hair bristling in the torchlight, his customary scowl on his face.

Minka threw herself into Mother's arms and burst into tears, and Lizzie felt her own lips trembling as she ran up to Father and let him pat her gently on the back.

"We feared the bears had got you," Father said. He tried to make it sound like he was joking, but the strain in his voice showed up scarlet red to Lizzie.

"We didn't even see any bears," she reassured Father. She didn't say anything about the wolves.

"The lost are found!" Dr. Śmigly said. "Come, let's leave this place. It gives me the jitters." She turned, her torch held high, and guided them along a wide path.

Stefan came up to Lizzie as they walked. "I told on you," he said. "I hope you're not too mad. I was scared."

"I'm not mad," she assured him. "It was a good thing to do. Are you angry at us? For leaving you like that?"

"Well, yes," Stefan admitted. "I was so mad at first! I couldn't believe you just left. But then I got worried, and when Pa started asking questions I couldn't think of what to say. So I told the truth–except about the goblins."

"I'm glad you did," Lizzie said.

"Was it bad? Were you afraid? Did you kill anyone?"

"Shh," Lizzie said. "We'll tell you everything later. But no, I didn't kill anyone."

"Rats!" Stefan said.

They emerged from the darkness of the trees into the lane, where the horizon was lightening just a tiny bit with the soft pink that signaled sunrise. Kosmy and several other donkeys grazed along the berm, hitched to their wagons.

"Look at you!" Stefan said, wide-eyed. Lizzie looked down at herself. Her skirt was ripped in several places, her underskirt mud-spattered. Her blouse sleeve was sliced open from the plant-teeth in the goblin house and dotted with bloodstains. Beside her, Minka stood awkwardly in her underclothes, and Jakob came up behind them, his trousers sliced to ribbons and his legs scratched and scabbing.

"Whatever possessed you, child?" Mother said fiercely to Minka, her relief giving way to anger. She held Minka at arm's length. "Whatever *happened*?"

"It was all my fault," Minka admitted.

"Stefan said you went to meet a boy—a boy! Oh Minka, what were you thinking?"

"I wasn't thinking," Minka said, low.

"It wasn't your fault," Lizzie said.

"And he wasn't a boy," Stefan jumped in. "He—"

Lizzie kicked him, hard.

"Ow! What? Why'd you—"

"He was grown, and way too old for Minka. And she saw that," Lizzie said, glaring at Stefan. He made a face back at her, but it was clear to Lizzie that he'd remembered: there was to be no mention of goblins, even now.

"And—why are you in your underskirt?" Mother said. "Where are your clothes? And where did you get that necklace?"

Tears spilled down Minka's face. "I—I was wearing my wedding dress," she admitted through sobs. "I took it off. And this locket was from him—from Emil." She reached up and gave the necklace a great yank. The chain broke. She threw it as hard as she could, into the underbrush. "Don't be angry with Lizzie and Jacob! Look how they came through the woods for me. Look what the thorns and briars did to them! And Emil–he was careless with his torch, and he started a fire, and we had to run. He's long gone, Mother, and I'll never see him again. I swear."

"And you, boy!" Jakob's father burst out. "What business d'ye have taking girls into the woods at night? What kind of behavior is that? Did I raise ye for that sort of thing?"

"It's none of *your* business, Pa, that's for sure," Jakob said calmly. "And you didn't raise me for much of anything, as far as I can tell. Ma raised me, and then I raised myself."

"Jakob was very brave," Lizzie protested, a little surprised at herself for speaking in front of so many people. But Jakob's father was being terribly unfair. "We might have been lost forever if he hadn't been there!"

Jakob's father let out a grunt of anger and said, "Rubbish!" He took a step toward his son, but Father held up a hand.

"We're all tired and overwrought," he said. "Let's not let our feelings get away from us. A night's sleep will make everything clearer."

Jakob's father snorted and spat, but he said nothing more.

Mistress Klara rubbed Lizzie's head before she could duck away and said, "You three are lucky you got found! When I heard you'd disappeared in the woods, we were all *that* worried. I've heard tales of children lost in the forest who never came out again—or who came out just a pile of bones to be buried by their poor old parents."

"Oo!" Stefan shivered with fearful delight. "Were they eaten by wild animals?"

"More likely starved," Dr. Śmigly said. "Or died of exposure. I remember a brother and sister—oh, years ago! Do you recall that, Mistress Klara?"

"I do," Mistress Klara said somberly.

"They went to find nuts—in Noc Forest in November, of all foolish times and places!—and it was two full days before the search party found them. They'd frozen to death, even though they'd come across a little shelter. Where was it they were found?"

"The ruined house," Mistress Klara said. Lizzie drew in a quick breath.

"A ruined house?" she said. "Where?"

"Oh, deep inside. A full day's walk at least. It's just a stone foundation, has been since long before my time. I heard it burned down a hundred years ago or more."

Lizzie and Jakob exchanged wide-eyed glances. A hundred years ago! But they'd seen the house, complete and intact, just hours before! Jakob seemed about to speak, so Lizzie gave him a quick, nearly imperceptible shake of the head. He nodded back.

"Why would anyone build a house in the middle of the forest?" he asked instead.

Mistress Klara shrugged. "I've no idea. Maybe the forest was smaller back then, or safer. At any rate, you should count yourselves lucky you were found so fast."

"Oh, we do," Lizzie said fervently. "We were very lucky!"

Mistress Klara gave Minka a hug. *"Well done, child!"* she whispered to Lizzie.

Then Father boosted Lizzie and Minka into the wagon. Jakob and Stefan climbed into their father's cart, and they set off back down the lane, calling their farewells to each other as the sun broke free of the horizon and bathed them with its dawn light.

CHAPTER 15

It was well after noon when Lizzie woke up. She wasn't sure where she was at first; the sunlight slanted through the tiny loft window at an unfamiliar angle, it was so late. She didn't remember arriving at the cottage, or changing into her nightdress, or climbing up to the loft. She stretched luxuriously, accidentally whacking Minka, who slept beside her.

Minka's eyes popped open. "Where are we? Are we home?" she asked immediately, panic on her face.

"Yes, we're home. We're in our own bed," Lizzie said, and Minka sighed with relief.

"So we are," she said. "Oh, Lizzie! What a terrible night." Her expression clouded over.

"It was pretty awful," Lizzie allowed.

"That fire!" Minka said. "And the wolves."

"It was scary. But we're all right. All of us. And the zduzses are gone.... At least I hope they are."

"Are they? Can we be sure?" Minka shuddered. "They were so dreadful. And Emil was one of them. Emil!" Her lower lip trembled.

"Yes," Lizzie said. "Are you sad? Will you miss him?"

"Sad?" Minka nodded, then shook her head. "I'm— oh, I don't even know. I suppose I'm sad. I thought he loved me. I thought I loved him! It was all like...like a kind of fever dream, I suppose. I'm angry. I'm ashamed."

"Ashamed?"

"I was so stupid! It's humiliating, that I was fooled like that. That I fell in love with—oh, I don't know— some kind of monster." She grimaced. "But I did. Just because he was nice to look at, and flattered me, and told me what I wanted to hear. And if I'd stayed, what would have happened?"

"I don't know," Lizzie said. "But it wasn't your fault. They were goblins. They had some sort of awful magic."

"I suppose they did," Minka allowed. "But they— or Emil, anyway—saw something in me that drew him to me, and drew me to him."

"Your unhappiness," Lizzie said. "I didn't know you were so unhappy." There was a pause, and Lizzie looked away.

"It's not because of you, Lizzie. It was never because of you."

"I know," Lizzie said. She did know, now.

The sisters climbed down the ladder. At the bottom, they turned and looked at each other. Minka burst out laughing.

"Look at us!" she cried, and Lizzie looked down at herself, at the scrapes on her arms, her dirt-streaked legs. She felt her tangled hair and rubbed her sleeve across her face. A smudge of soot came off on the white cotton. Minka looked even worse, straggle-haired and filthy. Lizzie giggled.

"Baths, girls!" Mother stood by the stove, heating an enormous pot of water. The idea of a hot bath was delicious—but not as delicious as the stack of naleśniki pancakes that sat warming on a plate on the stovetop.

"Can we eat first?" Lizzie asked. "I'm so hungry!"

"Eat," Mother said. "But quickly. You look a mess, and you reek of smoke."

The girls dug into their naleśniki. Before long, smears of jam mingled with the soot on their faces, and when they couldn't eat another bite, they took their turns bathing in the big wooden tub that was usually reserved for Saturday evenings. When they were scrubbed and dressed, Lizzie examined the place on her arm where the leaf in the goblin house had bitten her. It was much smaller than she'd feared—or it was healing very quickly. And the cut on her hand where the plum tree branch had gashed her was entirely gone.

"Look," Lizzie said, passing Minka the mirror. "Your hair is growing back! You look like a baby duck. And it's silver. It's so pretty!"

Minka ran her hand over the top of her head. "Thank goodness," she said. "Maybe it'll grow back curly. I always wanted curly hair." Lizzie rolled her eyes, and Minka laughed.

Mother told them Dr. Śmigly and Mistress Klara would be joining them for supper. "We wouldn't have known what to do without Mistress Klara," she said. "She showed us the path into Noc Forest. So at least we had an idea of where to look. Oh, girls, what were you thinking?" Her expression was at once angry and bewildered. When the sisters didn't speak, she added, "We *will* be talking about this, after our guests are gone. You cannot just run off into the forest with no explanation! And a young man? What if…" She stopped, unwilling to describe the possibilities she had imagined.

Lizzie and Minka exchanged a glance and nodded in resignation. It wasn't a talk they looked forward to.

Minka set bread to rise, and Lizzie made lopsided dumplings for the soup. Then Mother sent them outside to rest in the fresh air. Lizzie stopped short just outside the door.

"Look at the cherry tree!" she said. Its leaves had all turned brown and fallen, though autumn was still barely a hint in the air. Its branches looked withered, and the lichen that had grown on its trunk was crumbling. Lizzie reached out and pulled at a twig. It snapped off in her hand, dry and dead.

"Oh," Minka said softly, regretfully. She put out a hand to touch the trunk, then pulled it back.

"Did Emil really talk to you through that tree?" Lizzie asked.

"It seemed like he did," Minka said. "He told me things."

"What sorts of things?"

"The things he knew I wanted to hear. About how beautiful I was, how talented. And he told me I had to meet him in the forest. That's why I left."

"And he spied on us," Lizzie reminded her. "He heard us talking about our song."

Minka sighed. "Yes, he did." Then she pointed down the lane. "Look, there's Jakob!"

Lizzie squinted in the late-afternoon sun and saw Jakob in the distance. He raised a hand. Behind him, as always, was Stefan, hopping on one foot.

"Hello, Jakob," Minka said when they reached the girls.

Jakob smiled and scuffed a boot in the dust. "How are you feeling?"

"I'm better. Because of you, you and Lizzie. Listen, Jakob. I—well. Just—thank you. Thank you. And I'm sorry."

"Sorry for what?" Jakob said. "You didn't do anything wrong."

"I did, though," Minka said. "I put you both in danger."

Jakob thought about this, then nodded. "We're all right, though."

"Yes," Minka acknowledged. "We were lucky. But if I hadn't had you and Lizzie—I'd be gone. Dead, or worse."

"What's worse than dead?" Stefan asked. Nobody answered.

They sat under an old oak, enjoying the late-summer

warmth. It wasn't muggy and hot anymore. Lizzie could feel the cool breath of autumn in the air and see it in the gold-tinged sounds of the leaves rustling.

"The thing is..." Minka said after they'd been quiet awhile, "I've been thinking. What if they–the zduzses–try it again? I can't bear the idea of this happening to someone else."

"What can you do?" Lizzie asked.

"If someone had warned me, maybe I'd have thought twice about Emil."

"Would you have believed it if someone had told you, though?" Jakob said. "I mean, if you hadn't seen it–*them*–the goblins–well, it sounds awfully farfetched."

"I don't know," Minka said, pulling up grass with nervous fingers. "But I think I have to tell people. I need at least to try to make sure it doesn't happen again. To some other girl. Like Janina."

Janina, who had died. And Ada, who had died. And the girl from the north, who had died. How many more were there? And how many had *not* died, but been taken away forever?

Lizzie looked at Minka. "There were other girls, too, you know, besides Janina."

"There were?" Minka said. "How do you know?"

Lizzie described her day in Elza: the visits with the prorok, with Dr. Kluk, with the Babises. Minka was wide-eyed with surprise.

"You did all that, saw all those people? For me? To help me?"

"Well—yes."

"Oh, Lizzie," Minka said, her voice trembling. "In the house, before it burned, when you said you loved me—you meant it, didn't you?"

Lizzie stared at the ground. "Of course I did," she said, her voice low. "Didn't you know that?"

"I did," Minka said. "But I think I must have forgotten."

Lizzie could tell that Minka wanted to hug her. Reluctantly she leaned toward her sister. The hug lasted only a moment, and then Lizzie straightened up again.

"We should tell people about the zduszes," she said briskly. "I think you're right."

"They won't believe it," Jakob pointed out.

"Even if some people don't really believe it, or think it's a fairy tale of some kind, they'd be on the lookout. That way, if a girl sees a beautiful boy with beautiful fruit, she'll think of the story, and she'll be mindful. She'll know a boy who speaks sweet and looks sweet can't *be* sweet, if her friends and her sister hate him." She gave Minka a meaningful look.

"That's smart," Jakob said. Lizzie looked down, pleased at the compliment. "But Minka, wouldn't it be hard for you to tell what happened? I mean, it would sound..."

"Embarrassing?" Minka finished for him. "Humiliating? I suppose it would. Is that a good reason to stay quiet, though, if telling could save someone else?"

"No," Jakob said. "Of course not. You're very brave." He put a hand over Minka's, and she flushed and let it stay for a moment before pulling away.

"Hey, Lizzie," Stefan said as he tried to whittle a stick with his dull penknife.

"What?"

"What color is my voice?"

Lizzie blinked, surprised. She turned questioning eyes to Jakob.

"I'm sorry," Jakob said. "I told him. I was explaining what happened in the forest, and how we followed Minka—and he just got it out of me. You know how he is."

Lizzie smiled. "It's not a secret, I guess," she said. "I'm not ashamed of it."

"Why would it be a secret?" Stefan demanded.

"It's amazing! You are so lucky! It must be incredible to see all those colors. I wish I could do it."

Lizzie had never thought about it that way. "Sometimes it's incredible," she allowed. "But sometimes it's kind of horrible, if there's a lot of noise."

Stefan looked at her with sudden understanding. "Like someone yelling, or a thunderstorm?" he said. "Or—a big party in the Hall?"

"Exactly," Lizzie said. He nodded.

"I'll try to be quieter," he said, and Lizzie laughed. "But still, what color is my voice?"

"It's a kind of deep red. Like a ripe tomato."

"Really?" Stefan was fascinated. "Hello!" he called out, standing up to try to see his words as they emerged from his mouth. "Hello, hello!" But of course he didn't see anything. Disappointed, he sat back down.

"Did your father let you go this afternoon to come visit us?" Minka asked Jakob.

He shook his head. "No, we just left."

"He yelled," Stefan noted. "But Jakob said we didn't have to worry."

"No?" Minka's voice was gentle.

"I've decided to get a place in Elza," Jakob said. "I'm taking Stefan with me. I'm done with school now, and Stef can go to school in town."

"But what will you do for work?"

"Dr. Śmigly has found me an apprenticeship with Dr. Lis. He's one of the town doctors."

"Oh, Jakob, that's wonderful!" Minka clapped her hands together. "But we'll miss seeing you."

"It's not that far. And I'll be back," Jakob assured her. "I promised Father I'd help with the harvest. I don't want to leave him alone—not completely, anyway. Not yet."

Minka sighed. "I wish I could find something like that, something I really want to do." She lay back in the grass and stared up the sky. "Something like what Emil promised."

"Love?" Jakob said, low. Stefan snickered.

"No! I mean, yes, someday. But not for a while. I've had my fill of that for now. It was more—the freedom. The idea of doing what I love."

"Painting," Lizzie said.

"Yes, painting. Oh, he made it all sound possible—like I could paint landscapes, and wall frescoes, and portraits, and sell my work to rich people. I don't know why I believed him."

"He was a zdusze," Lizzie pointed out. "I suppose that's what they do—they deceive people."

"You know," Jakob said, "Dr. Śmigly is on the

town council. And she told me awhile back that they were looking for someone to decorate the Hall. For the renovation."

Minka sat up and stared at him. "Really? What kind of decoration were they thinking of?"

"I don't know. You'd have to ask her."

"Oh, Minka!" Lizzie exclaimed. "Imagine painting the walls of the Town Hall! You would do such a wonderful job!"

Minka shook her head. "They would never choose me. They'll bring in someone from far away, someone who's a real artist."

Lizzie scowled. "Don't say that. You *are* a real artist," she said firmly. "Bring them some of your work. They'll choose you, I know they will."

Minka looked at her, and Lizzie could see her eyes glistening. "I could try," she said.

"You could," Lizzie agreed.

"There's no guarantee that they'd take me."

"No, no guarantee."

"But I could try anyway."

"You could," Lizzie said again, and smiled at her sister. "Who knows? If you do one job, more could follow!"

"We'll be taking a cart to town tomorrow, for our

move," Jakob said. "I could bring some of your work to show the council. Or you could come with us."

"I could," Minka said. She smiled at Jakob, so brightly that he flushed in its warmth.

"Is that Mistress Klara?" Stefan said, jumping up and pointing down the lane. "What's she doing here?"

"Mother invited her for supper," Minka told him. "And Dr. Śmigly. And I'm sure she'd like you both to come, too."

"Mmm, your mother's cooking!" Stefan crowed. "Did she make a babka? A chocolate one?"

"Maybe," Lizzie teased him. "You'll have to stay to find out."

"And we'll tell them at supper," Minka said. "We'll tell them everything that happened. Even if they won't believe it."

Lizzie nodded. "Everything. To save the other girls."

"To save the other girls," Minka repeated.

They got to their feet and watched as Mistress Klara walked toward them and Dr. Śmigly appeared from the other direction. Stefan's always-sticky hand found its way into Lizzie's, and she squeezed.

Minka gave a deep sigh, and Lizzie let go of Stefan and put a hand on her sister's arm. "It won't be so very bad," she said, echoing the reassuring words she'd heard from Minka so often. "And don't worry. I'll be right there with you."

The promise must have comforted Minka in a way that it had never quite managed to comfort Lizzie, for she gave her sister a smile and nodded. "I know you will," she said warmly, and they headed into the house to greet their guests.

Acknowledgments

My deepest thanks to:

Mora Couch, for helping to make this story so very creepy

Jennifer Laughran, for doing all the hard stuff

Shani Soloff, for cheering me on and putting me back together

Debra and Arnie Cardillo, for giving voice(s) to my words

Denise Hancock (aka Pooh), dearly loved and greatly missed

And always and most of all, my husband Phil Sicker, for all those walks up Clark Hill Road where the ideas live